I TOTALLY WOULD HAVE walked right by, but Oliver was sitting out front on a bench, playing his guitar, and he called to me.

I was not faking a startled reaction.

He patted the seat beside him.

I hesitated.

He waited.

I crossed my arms.

He strummed a chord and sang softly, "Quinn Avery stood on my sidewalk today, trying to decide—walk . . . or stay. . . ."

I couldn't help smiling a little.

"Stay," he said softly.

Novels by Rachel Vail

WONDER

DO-OVER

EVER AFTER

DARING TO BE ABIGAIL

NEVER MIND!

IF WE KISS

YOU, MAYBE: *The Profound Asymmetry
of Love in High School*

LUCKY

GORGEOUS

BRILLIANT

The Friendship Ring:

IF YOU ONLY KNEW

PLEASE, PLEASE, PLEASE

NOT THAT I CARE

WHAT ARE FRIENDS FOR?

POPULARITY CONTEST

FILL IN THE BLANK

BRILLIANT

Rachel Vail

HARPER TEEN
An Imprint of HarperCollinsPublishers

To Zachary

HarperTeen is an imprint of HarperCollins Publishers.

Brilliant
Copyright © 2010 by Rachel Vail
All rights reserved. Printed in the United States of America.
No part of this book may be used or reproduced in any manner whatsoever
without written permission except in the case of brief quotations
embodied in critical articles and reviews. For information address
HarperCollins Children's Books, a division of
HarperCollins Publishers, 10 East 53rd Street,
New York, NY 10022.
www.epicreads.com

Library of Congress Cataloging-in-Publication Data.
Vail, Rachel.
Brilliant / Rachel Vail. — 1st ed.
    p. cm.
Summary: Sixteen-year-old Quinn struggles to maintain her image as a brilliant, good
girl when her mother's major error at work leads to financial and legal troubles that turn
Quinn's and her younger sisters' world upside-down.
  ISBN 978-0-06-089051-3
  [1. Conduct of life—Fiction. 2. Mothers and daughters—Fiction. 3. Family problems—
Fiction. 4. Sisters—Fiction.] I. Title.
PZ7.V1916Bri 2010   2009039672
[Fic]—dc22   CIP

Typography by Joel Tippie
11 12 13 14 15 LP/BV 10 9 8 7 6 5 4 3 2 1
❖
First paperback edition, 2011

1

SHE TOOK MY ROOM AWAY.

Not literally, of course. The room is still there, through the door from the hall, across from my younger sisters' rooms, where it was this morning when I left. It's just not mine anymore, not really, not recognizably, because my brilliant mother, master of the universe, Porsche-in-woman-form, had my red room painted white while I was at camp orientation today.

She didn't think it would matter to me.

My red, red room has been whitewashed.

She actually didn't think it would matter to me. I am prepared to believe the truth of that statement. It's a compliment, really. She thought it wouldn't matter to me, so it can't. I can't let it.

We're moving soon anyway (which is a big part of why it shouldn't—doesn't—matter to me), and apparently people are afraid of red rooms.

"Why would people be afraid of red rooms?" I asked her, instead of, *How could you do this to me? Without even asking me?*

She shook her head over the disbelief we shared about the numbskull Others, the rest of the world who were not Avery Women, not Us, people who were afraid of red rooms. "Hard to fathom how they function at all."

"The redness of my room was literally scaring people away from buying our house?" I mumbled to her, standing by her side in the hall, peering into the white room that used to be my room.

She laughed her irresistible laugh and said, "Exactly. Unbelievable."

"I liked it red," I managed.

"That's because you're extraordinary, Quinn." She threw her arm around my shoulder and gave it a quick squeeze. "You're the best," she whispered, then kissed my hair and strode off in her smooth, long-legged way toward her room, checking her BlackBerry as she went.

Even Porsches have blind spots.

Weird that before we moved in, when my room was white, I could see it red exactly as it would be and eventually became. Now, after four years of living in it red and only like half an hour of whiteness, I cannot for the life of me summon the exact tint of red it was, or remember if that molding a foot from the ceiling was red like the walls beneath it or white like the section above. I don't know.

I don't know.

Maybe it's the paint fumes but I feel seriously off.

How can I not picture my room as it was this morning?

We were the first family ever to live in this house. We walked through it, all five of us, before the doorways had doors, when all the walls were still toxic-smelling white, and crinkly brown paper was taped in runways on the floors. It was mostly just beams and plasterboard then. It echoed.

Mom kept murmuring, *Beautiful*. What I was thinking was *Huge*. It looked big enough for ten families but absurd for just the five of us. We walked around with our arms bumping into one another's, in a tight family clump. Allison chose her bedroom first. It was the biggest one, the one with the huge walk-in closet with double doors. She was ready with multiple arguments, geared up to fight.

I told her it was fine; she could have that room.

Phoebe said she didn't care which of the other two rooms she got. She was only eight. It was almost impossible for anyone to deny her anything, then or still, even if she didn't ask for it or know she wanted it. I gave her the bigger of the rooms, the one closer to Mom and Dad. I knew she'd like both of those qualities of it.

Later that day, when we were back in our old, suddenly cramped and cruddy house, Mom and Dad each caught me alone and whispered that they were proud of how generous I was being about choosing bedrooms at the new house. Such a good girl. I was grateful for the praise, but I was fooling only them, not myself: I knew it wasn't generosity inspiring me.

If we had to move here, I wanted that room, this room, my room. As soon as I saw it, I knew that I'd ask to have it painted red, even though blue was and remains my favorite color. It surprised everybody, which I don't usually do. I'm obviously not somebody who'd have a red room. But I could just see it painted red with bright white trim as soon as I walked into it. I knew in that first instant that this was my room.

I let everybody think I was selfless, though.

I liked that my room faced east, so I would get the morning light. Even then, four years ago, when I was an awkward and introverted twelve-and-a-half-year-old, I preferred to be the first one to see the new day. It gave me a feeling of control.

Or it could be that I had read something about Islamic culture that stuck with me.

The other part that I appreciated about my room was that it faced front. I have always liked knowing who is coming or going, and despite what my sisters may think, I don't just mean Oliver.

Oliver.

I know, I know. But he is perfect, and though he has only polite interest in me at most, it is hard to let go of

4

fantasies even when you are a realist and almost seventeen.

When I first heard my parents arguing in whispers about
whether we were going to lose the house, I wasn't scared.
Instead I was overwhelmingly tempted to run downstairs
and explain to them the absurdity of that construction: We
can't lose this house. It is huge and immovable, solid now.
The house will lose us, if anything.

But of course that wasn't the point (grammar is so
rarely the point, sadly), and wouldn't change the point,
would only reveal my eavesdropping and make my parents
coo and reassure, or maybe look at me in that tilted way
they sometimes do, like, *Are you delusional or just odd?*

So I said nothing. As usual.

Sometime in the near future we'll move, but already
right now my room isn't my room anymore. It will soon
be somebody else's room, with somebody else's stuff in
the closet and somebody else looking out the east-facing
window to see who is coming and who is going, and maybe
wishing that he would once, just once please look up at this
window as he leaves. Someone else will gaze into the full-
length mirror on the back of my bathroom door and not
see me reflected there but herself.

But for now this room isn't somebody else's yet.

It's just not mine anymore, either.

Soon I'll be gone, and all the possible me's, all the
things I imagined doing in this house, in this room, won't

exist anymore. I'll never have sex in this room. I'll never climb out this window onto the ledge and look down at a boy who is looking up at me, like Romeo, with love in his eyes. I won't finish growing up in this room.

We won't be the last family to live in this house.

We will be replaced.

Re-placed.

Placed again, but in a different place.

I am sitting here alone in the doorway of my toxic-white-paint-fume-infested, east-facing room confronting the awful truth that I am completely, devastatingly re-placeable.

I DIDN'T INTEND TO STEAL her shoes, and the fact that I sort of actually did steal her shoes was definitely not about revenge or retribution.

I just couldn't get myself over the threshold into my room. After sitting there thinking for a while, I realized what the problem was. Clearly I was uncomfortable about how things had been handled and needed to talk with Mom about it. That seemed like a fully reasonable response, a mature way to handle things—discuss it, air my grievance, persuade her that she had handled it badly. Even if it didn't turn my room red, well, maybe an apology would help me deal with it better than sitting in the hall, silently cursing.

The thing is—well, one minor thing is—I don't curse. I don't even curse inside the private confines of my own mind. I had decided back in ninth grade that cursing is a sign of either laziness or poorly developed vocabulary. But there, as I sat outside my ex-room, with curses raging in my brain, it occurred to me that maybe I had always been a wrongheaded prig about curses, and that in fact there was a place in my vocabulary, at least my silent thought vocabulary, for an occasional expletive.

Or maybe, judging by the crazy combinations of words chasing one another through my head, referring to body parts, biological functions, and questionable circumstances of parentage, Allison's brain had been transplanted into my skull.

No. I am Quinn, not crazy, raging Allison; I am the oldest, the one who handles things well and doesn't curse. I must get a grip.

So I just took a few deep breaths and walked down the hall to Mom's room to discuss what had happened. As I got closer I considered various ways of beginning the conversation, such as, for instance, *Mom, maybe you could have discussed the painting of my room with me ahead of time, instead of just, "Surprise! We have erased you! Now cope with it!"*

No, that's not what happened. This is just a difficult time, I reminded myself, because of the Situation; I have to be patient with myself, and my sisters and Dad, of course, but most of all with Mom. She is counting on me. Patient and also vigilant.

Which is why Allison and I hooked up the baby monitor back in May: so we could spy on our parents as they talked with my mother's spherical lawyer about what they called, with capitalization and italics in their voices, *the Situation*.

Of course, I already knew what had happened. Mom had gotten fired.

It's not like it was a mystery. She had told us over chicken and broccoli at dinner the day after it happened. She was, as always, very factual and calm and precise about it. No hysteria from Mom. We all, especially I, try to live up to her high standard of handling things well and unemotionally. We finished our chicken and our broccoli, cleared our plates, and went up to our rooms to do our homework. The next morning at dawn, when only the two of us were up, Mom told me that she was counting on me to help my sisters cope. I said, "Of course, Mom. Don't worry about that. Don't worry about us."

The fact that she was fired did not change my feelings about her one bit. I told Allison and Phoebe that it was actually amazing she lasted as long as she did in that place, with all the knives sharpened against her.

My mother started out as a junior assistant at Excelsior Capital after she went to business school at night when we were little. She found out really quickly that she was good at making money, better than the guys she worked for, better than she'd been at anything else in her life.

("Other than being a mom," Phoebe always prompted her at this point in her story. Mom would blink twice, focusing on her youngest child's upturned face, and then answer, "Thank you, Phoebe. What a sweet thing to say." She seemed surprised by the interruption every time, and maybe she actually was.)

She made a daring gamble as soon as she had the chance at Excelsior. She "went to the edge" is the expression she uses, but I am sure it is a figurative edge. She basically gambled a huge amount of money and won.

Her picture was on the front page of the *Wall Street Journal*. It was the kind of picture that is called a dot picture, because instead of a photograph or drawing, there is a likeness made pointillistically by a computer. Although Seurat has nothing to worry about, this is apparently quite a big deal in the business world. Dad bought six copies of the paper that day, and a big bouquet of stargazer lilies to hand her when she walked in the door. My sisters and I were dancing around singing, "Hooray for Mommy!" I made her a pop-up congratulations card and let Allison and Phoebe sign it, too, even though they hadn't helped, and it had taken all of my ingenuity and tape.

The only person we knew at that point who'd had her picture in the newspaper was Liz Anne Montgomery, and that was for falling down a sewer hole and subsequently getting rescued by two firefighters with a rigged seat made of rope. Liz Anne Montgomery, who was an otherwise unnoticed child with unfortunately trimmed bangs, was a celebrity around school for a full week after that. She had to use crutches because of getting thirteen stitches and a sprain in her knee; we all jostled to get chosen to carry her books and lunch box for her from our classroom to art or the lunchroom.

Liz Anne Montgomery's picture was just in the local paper, not the *Wall Street Journal*, which was a serious paper, for adults only, no advice columns or comics, no frills except the dot pictures.

Also, realistically, falling down a sewer is not that impressive a feat, even for a chubby second grader. Liz Anne Montgomery faded from the spotlight once the crutches were gone, and her family moved to Ohio (it might have been Iowa) by the end of the year.

But Mom had apparently achieved something incredibly impressive to get her picture in the paper, and the phone didn't stop ringing that night, even after ten, long after we'd gone to bed full of ice cream and pride.

We weren't sure exactly what it was she'd done. We could tell by her face that it was big, and great.

It was soon after the dot picture that we got our new house, and the grand piano Mom bought for Dad to take up some room in the vast emptiness of the living room, and maybe also some of his time, because while she was out late with clients or on business trips, he would play the piano. It sounded much fuller than the upright that came with us from the old house and is now in the back left corner of our basement, with three lacrosse sticks and five bent or too-short ski poles stacked on top of it, the hinged door closed over its stained keys.

But just like he had in our old house with the upright, each night at bedtime Dad played some Beatles tunes, the bits of Beethoven's Ninth that he could remember, and finally "Summertime" from the opera *Porgy and Bess*. I would fall asleep every night to the reassuring sounds of the unrecognizable old songs he played softly after "Summertime."

The Situation seems in some ways like a mirror image of that dot-picture time. Mom made a huge gamble and everything changed as a result.

The dot-picture time, Mom got a new job title. She took a day off to buy new clothes, mostly Armani, and five pairs of impossibly beautiful pumps from Neiman Marcus to take the place of her old Frye boots. My sisters and I claimed the shoe boxes for dioramas. Sometimes we snuck into her closet and, breathing her perfume off her camisoles, tried on her shoes. They were so big, and the heels so high, we would tumble in heaps on top of one another. It felt daring and naughty and exhilarating trying on Mom's shoes. I was the one who always stopped the giggling before we got caught, and lined the shoes back up so nobody would know what we'd done.

We moved to this house later that spring, and started swimming in our own pool instead of the town pool and playing tennis on our own tennis court instead of the concrete court behind the high school. We each had our own room. I got a laptop and started taking piano lessons from the mom of a genius boy Dad had taught in kindergarten who skipped first grade he was so smart and was, by then, already in high school and already had those knee-weakening sexy eyes. I practiced every afternoon on the new piano, which was in fact grand, much too grand for the tinkling little sounds I could produce on it. Late at night my sisters and I could spy from the banister of the front stairway and catch Mom and Dad dancing in the still-empty-except-for-the-piano living room and sometimes they made out, which made us feel weird but also safe. We got a stern housekeeper named Agnes and a stylish nanny named Gosia, because Mom was working even longer hours. We went to Europe for the last two weeks of summer for the first time, a new Avery tradition. When we returned, our old Subaru went to Gosia; Mom bought a black Jeep for Dad, and for herself a red Porsche.

This summer we're not going to Europe. Our housekeeper, Agnes, was fired one morning in May while we were in school, so we never got to say good-bye to her. Our nanny, Gosia, seeing the writing on the wall, got a different job that will start July 7. We're spending the two weeks' notice she gave us noticing her, saying good-bye to her. I'm not sure which way is worse but I think maybe the drawn-out version.

Okay, maybe good-bye just sucks any way you slice it.

I'm going to spend this summer very prestigiously

working at a camp for underprivileged kids. Like all the other counselors, whom I met today at orientation, I am (or at least have been) overprivileged, and this job, while fulfilling on its own merits, was also designed, not just coincidentally, to help me get into an elite college eventually, so that I could continue on my overprivileged path. The irony was lost on nobody, especially me.

Yet with all my hyperawareness of both irony and Mom, I am not sure what it was that Mom did this time, either, to cause the Situation. But I could tell by her face even back in May that it was big, and did not work out well at all.

Instead of a jumbo-size bouquet of stargazer lilies and multiple deliveries from Neiman's, this time, Mom got a lawyer. And a real estate agent who told her that people will not buy a house, especially in this economy, that has a red room in it.

I took two more deep breaths, having calmed myself down enough to ensure that I would not race in and burst out crying and cursing nonsensically at my mother, and knocked on her bedroom door.

No answer.

I tried the knob. It twisted easily and I opened the door. "Mom?" I heard the water running in her bathroom. I stepped one foot into her room and stopped, one foot on each side—my right foot on the soft white carpeting of my parents' room, the other on the hardwood floor of the hall.

"Mom?" I called again. Either of my sisters would have

walked right in, no hesitation. Well, Allison would have stalked in, demanding something, ready to argue. Phoebe would have wandered in, innocent and sweet, oblivious, entitled. And me? Well, normally I would have just waited to talk to her later, if she was in the shower.

Instead I called her name again as I straddled the threshold, thinking about the metaphor I was unwillingly making of myself.

"What are you doing?" Phoebe asked, suddenly beside me.

I jumped.

"Sorry," she said. "I didn't mean to startle you. Why are you standing here rocking back and forth in Mom's doorway?"

"Just . . . just thinking," I said.

Phoebe smiled. "Okay, well, cool. Have fun with that, then."

"Thanks," I said. "Did you need something?"

"No, it's all good," she said, backing away like I was some kind of lovable but whack-job genius. "You just keep thinking there. Didn't mean to interrupt your rhythm, or whatever."

"No worries," I said, just as I heard the water shut off. "Mom?"

"Quinn?" she called from the bathroom.

"Yes," I answered, rooted to the spot. "Mom? I was—"

"Oh, good, Quinn. Could you bring me the dress that's

on the bed there? I meant to bring it in here with me to steam out the wrinkles. Quickly, Quinn?"

Ah, the one thing sure to uproot me: obedience. I flew to her bed, where a white summer sundress was splayed, unwrinkled, on a hanger. I brought it to her in the bathroom, where she was wrapped in one of her superthick terry bath sheets, her hair dark wet, water drops dripping from her long eyelashes.

"Thanks, sweetie," she said. "Just hang it right there on the hook. Great." She bent over and rubbed her hair with a smaller, matching towel.

I turned around, dismissed. As I was walking through her bedroom, I saw that her shoe closet doors were splayed open. Her shoes were lined up in neat rows, like spectators at a concert. Her neat gene had skipped me and gone right to Allison. I lingered in front of the shoes and looked at each pair, not touching at first, just looking. The names signed inside them sounded like music, like foreign language lyrics to an aria of longing:

Valentino Jimmy Choo
Louboutin Miu Miu
Manolo Blahnik Ferragamo
Rangoni Dolce & Gabbana

I traced my fingers over some of them, but not the black patent-leather ones, because I remembered the fingerprints my sisters and I had desperately rubbed off against the carpet. No evidence, I thought. I reached toward the back. My favorites were there, strange favorites for a girl who only wears silent sneakers and feels ludicrously self-proclaiming in ballet flats or loafers, but they were my secret absolute favorites nevertheless. I pulled them out. They were new, never worn; I hadn't tottered around with my sisters in these—bold fuchsia stilettos in smooth, cool satin with a little space in front for toes to peek out under a sparkly rhinestone ring—the sexiest shoes I'd ever seen.

I held the pair of them in my hands, weighing them for the moment, thinking.

Then I shut her closet and dashed out of her room, the shoes dangling from my guilty fingers, and crashed into Allison in the hall.

"What the hell?" she demanded.

"Allison," I said, trying to hide the shoes casually behind my back.

"Oh, it's my fault? You come flying around corners without looking and what—what did I do now?"

I blinked twice. "I don't know," I said slowly, thinking a mile a minute. "What did you do?"

"Fine, forget it," she said. "Sorry if we can't all be as Zen-perfect as you. Because I swear, if they painted my room? I mean, did she even ask you first?"

"No," I said.

"And it's just . . . you're fine with that?"

"No," I admitted. Behind me I heard Mom open her shoe closet.

"But you just deal. I know, I know," Allison rambled on, volume increasing. "The Situation. Right, but you know what? If it were my room? I would not be all blissed out like you."

"Hey, girls?" Mom called from her room.

I had to get out of there. Her shoes were dangling from my fingertips. What if these were the ones she was looking for?

"I'm not blissed," I whispered to Allison, nudging her toward our rooms, away from Mom.

"Girls?" Mom repeated.

"I can't believe you painted Quinn's room!" Allison yelled toward Mom. "That is the crappiest—"

"Allison, don't start, please," Mom yelled.

"Let's go," I growled at Allison, hinting urgently.

But Allison yanked her arm away from my grasp. "If you are too la-la-la to speak up for yourself, somebody has to," she said, and stormed into Mom's room. "If you ever did that to me, I swear I'd tear the house down by hand! How could you?"

"Allison Avery," Mom barked at her. "I did not ask your opinion. Now you march your obnoxious self out of my room and quit trying to butt in where you don't belong. It's Quinn's room, and she, thank goodness, is mature and reasonable, so . . ."

I didn't hear the rest. I closed the door of the room that had been mine but was now a weird avant-garde-movie-set shiny white, and leaned against the still-sticky door until my heart returned to a life-compatible rhythm.

Then I yanked out my underwear drawer. I quickly tucked Mom's loud, sexy, out-of-place shoes in there, way in the back, beneath some old bras, and closed the drawer.

I figured I'd just return the shoes when Mom was out sometime, and the whole shoe-stealing incident would be past, just a weird little blip in my excellent, smooth, admirable life.

I SLEPT IN THE GUEST ROOM because of the fumes, and when I woke up the next morning for camp, I had no idea where I was. By the time I figured it out, I had only ten minutes to get ready before my best friend, Jelly, was due to pick me up. I dashed through my room, pausing only microscopically at the blinding whiteness on my way to my bathroom, where I brushed my teeth and flipped my hair into a ponytail, clonking my head on the corner of the sink in the process, which caused me to choke violently on the toothpaste. I was on my way down the stairs when I heard Jelly's distinctively tooting beep.

My parents and Allison weren't around. Phoebe was trying to convince Gosia that Allison's flip-flops belonged to her, and also to please get the dirt stains off them somehow before Allison woke up and saw. While Gosia was explaining in her patient, lightly accented voice that dirt stains are almost impossible to remove, I said good-bye to them and stopped the door from slamming behind me.

Jelly had rap music on loud. I turned it down. "You can't actually like that stuff," I said as she backed her huge car expertly down my driveway.

"I don't," she admitted. "But how cliché would it be if I only listened to classical, right?"

"If the shoe fits . . ." I started, but that reminded me about the stolen shoes that were hiding in my underwear drawer. Would they fit me? Probably not, and it wouldn't matter. I wasn't ever actually going to wear them anyway! So I shrugged and leaned back in my seat.

"Even if the shoe fits, you don't have to wear it," Jelly argued, bopping unconvincingly to the beat. "There are other shoes that'll fit, too."

Jelly (whose birth-cert name is Jill, but nobody ever uses anything but the name her older brother, Erik, gave her at birth: Jelly) is what she calls Jew-panese (her mom is Jewish, her dad Japanese), and so, according to her, has a double dose of You Are Such a Grind, genetically. The fact that she is also an actual grind made shirking the label that much harder.

"Maybe we should just embrace the fact that we are nerds," I suggested, as she flew down the entrance ramp onto the highway, while surreptitiously checking her mirrors.

"No, Quinn," she insisted, opening all the windows simultaneously with the long fingers of her left hand, while maintaining a cool eight miles over the speed limit (she had read on a website that police radar is set to nine miles above the speed limit). "Don't embrace nerd status. Just because we study hard for every test and floss our teeth doesn't mean we can't also have a hidden wild side. We actually might! Do not go gentle into that nerd night. Rage, rage, against the dying of the possibility we might seem cool to somebody someday."

"Okay, okay." I smiled and leaned my head on the shoulder strap of my seat belt. "That's really likely, by the way."

She smiled her lopsided smile. "Maybe to somebody extremely minimally observant."

I considered telling her about my room, but I honestly just didn't want to deal with thinking about it. Eight hours of being away from home felt, for the first time ever, like a gift, or a vacation.

The underprivileged campers weren't coming until the next day, so we overprivileged staff were doing team-building kinds of stuff, which I was dreading, but which ended up being less stupid than I'd feared. Luckily Jelly and I were placed together, counselors of the Hawks, along with a girl named Adriana Dominguez.

Jelly and I shot a look at each other when we met her. She was stunning even before she smiled, but when she turned that wide grin on us, it was hard not to be dazzled. She's the kind of person you really don't want to like:

too beautiful, fashionable, confident. But she was, to add insult to injury, really friendly and nice, too.

She was going into senior year at the private school named Chadwick, up-county from us. When we went to get water during a break, Jelly said, "I think I may be allergic to Adriana. She is too flawless; it hurts my eyes."

"Maybe she'll turn out to be minimally observant," I suggested.

At least that made Jelly laugh.

Later in the day, when we were slumped on the hill listening to the music counselors do their end-of-camp-day songs, I blurted out that my parents are selling our house so they painted my room white.

Jelly's jaw dropped. "Wait, what?"

"That sucks," Adriana said, holding out a pack of gum. I took a piece. Jelly didn't even seem to notice; she was staring so hard at me.

"Yeah," I agreed. "Sucks." I folded the gum into my mouth. I almost never chew gum.

"You're moving?" Jelly asked. "Quinn, what?"

"Just downsizing," I said, trying to sound casual and not choke on the gum while talking. "You know, the economy."

"Yeah," Adriana said. "Your dad lose his job?"

"Mom," I said.

Jelly sucked in her perfect rosebud lips. I hadn't said anything to her about Mom, but I figured she knew anyway. The fact that she didn't ask anything confirmed that. For all I knew, there was stuff about it in the papers. Jelly read them; I didn't. Especially now.

"What does your father do?" Adriana asked.

"He's a kindergarten teacher."

"Really?"

"Yeah," I said. "Why?"

"So your mom is the money?"

I shrugged. "Well, was."

Adriana nodded. "Huh."

"What?" I asked.

"Nothing," she said, and flashed that smile again. "Just . . . different. Must be hard on your dad, you know, emasculating, all that. You know how guys are."

"No," I protested. "It's not—"

"Well," Adriana interrupted, throwing one arm over my shoulder and the other over Jelly's, like we were her longtime best buds. "If the home front sucks, we'll have to make sure the rest of your summer doesn't, right, Jelly?"

"Absolutely," Jelly agreed quietly. "You're not moving away, though, right?"

I shook my head and spit my gum into my hand. My jaw was already exhausted.

"I'll find us some fun, for sure," Adriana was saying, meanwhile standing up and brushing the grass off the back of her short cutoffs. Her gauzy shirt came down almost to the bottoms of them, and her thin multicolored bangles clanked cheerfully as she whipped her long billowy curls over her right shoulder. Her nail polish was complicated. I was trying to figure out what was drawn on her nails when I realized she was squinting down at us. "You guys aren't going out with anybody already, are you?"

Jelly and I both shook our nerdy heads.

"Excellent," Adriana said. "Blank slates."

THAT NIGHT, WHILE I WAS fast asleep in my/not-my room, Allison was suddenly there, too, in my bed, whispering furiously to me. I was nodding at her before my eyes were open, *shhh*ing her, trying to hold on to the remnants of my dream.

Oliver was in it. Something nice was happening, maybe a boat? A canoe. We were together in a green canoe with wooden oars in our hands and no lifejackets on. Were we on the lake in camp? But wait, there's a strict lifejackets rule at camp. And there was a fire, maybe a campfire but maybe it was a forest fire, but we weren't in the forest; we were in a canoe, on a lake; maybe we were escaping from the forest fire, escaping by canoe. But no, that didn't make any sense; Oliver wasn't even working at my camp, so where were we . . . ?

As soon as you try to apply logic to a dream it gets annoyed and pops like the soap bubble it is. I opened my eyes and tried to focus on my gorgeous, stressed-out sister's furious face, still wishing I could get back into that canoe.

"They're fighting," she was whispering. "Well, not fighting exactly, but, like, whispering and then getting louder and then nothing at all and then whispering again, you know? Like fighting but not fighting really, just kind of discussing while stressed out and thinking but not positive that we're asleep?"

"Who?" I managed, my eyes drifting closed again. I could smell the forest fire or campfire again; I was near it. If I could go right back to sleep, the dream might still be lingering, with Oliver behind me in the canoe. . . .

"Quinn, what, are you kidding or are you the stupidest frigging genius ever? Them! Mom and Dad. And what you said totally isn't true, Quinn; I'm serious."

This is the way Allison always talks, and even when I am fully conscious it is sometimes hard to keep afloat on the whitewater churning of her emotional tirades, canoe or no canoe.

"Okay," I said, rubbing my eyes. "Okay."

"Okay, you agree you were lying, or okay, you are finally conscious?"

"Um," I answered.

"Because she totally did it."

"Who? Mom? Did what?" I almost asked, *Started the forest fire?* But I had crossed just far enough into consciousness that I realized the forest fire was in my dream, was probably something Freudian about my apparently undying crush on Oliver. Monday nights were always rough that way, because my piano lesson was on Tuesdays. I yawned to block questions about my dreamworld out of the conversation, then asked, more annoyed than I meant to sound, "What are you talking about, Al? It's one in the morning."

Allison rolled her eyes at me. They still had remnants of smudgy black eyeliner on them. Allison had in the past couple of months emerged from her long, petulant, frown-filled hibernation in awkward adolescence as a head-turningly gorgeous girl. People literally turned their heads and stared at her now, and not (anymore) because she was throwing a tantrum. Well, not always, anymore. She wasn't pretty, really. I was, if anything, more of a pretty girl, or I always had been when we were little. I'm not saying I was any great beauty even back then. I mean pretty like fine, okay, pleasing. That was me. Allison was stunning suddenly. That's the word adults whispered about her. The boys throughout the high school used the excellent SAT vocab word *hot* instead, including the absolute hottest guy in *my* grade, who dogged Allison for a month before she deigned to start going out with him.

"What happened?" I asked her slowly, hoping to erase some of the nastiness that had menaced my last attempt, and also to hand off some bit of calm, which she desperately needed, as always.

She rolled her gray eyes again. "I just told you," she whispered. "Were you even listening?"

I knew that if I just sat still and silent, Allison would repeat whatever crisis she thought was brewing and had apparently told me in detail while I was fast asleep, escaping fires in a canoe with Oliver. As it was occurring to me that Dr. Freud would not need to be woken from the dead to interpret that most obvious cliché of a dream, it turned out I was right. Allison launched back into her crisis.

Allison was once again convinced—and trying to convince me—that despite all the evidence I'd marshaled, Mom had *not* been scapegoated by the jerk men on her team. Despite the fact that they are a *team*, and make decisions as a team, despite the fact that no trades or decisions can be made except with at least three of them signing off on the decision, Allison was convinced that Mom somehow managed to get around all the safeguards and invest millions (literally many millions—we had heard a bunch of different figures, but the one that kept recurring was $214 million) in a company, Galen, that, rather than curing cancer, like Mom thought it was about to do, was actually skidding down a steep hill toward bankruptcy.

As usual, I tried to calm Allison down. I tried to explain the structure of the hedge fund (as if I understood it myself) and why it was impossible, implausible, ridiculous to imagine Mom could have made $214 million disappear all by herself.

"She was a woman in the boys' locker room," I

explained. "You remember I did that report on women last year, on what happened when they first let women into the military, the firefighters' union, and even men's colleges? The first women were subjected to all kinds of brutality, scapegoating, and worse. . . ."

"Yeah," Allison grunted. "Except I am not talking about your damn homework, Quinn. I am talking about Mom. And maybe she did deal with a lot of that, whatever, misery . . ."

"Misogyny," I corrected, in spite of myself, not wanting to be a prig, but it was the middle of the night, so my social defenses were weak. "Irrational hatred of women."

"Whatever!" Allison sprang off my bed to pace around my cluttered room. "What I am saying," she whispered, "is that Mom is the one on the line here, not because the other guys are jerks, which they probably are. But because she did something way bad."

I flopped back down on my pillow. "You just hate her."

"Fine." Allison stalked toward my door.

I propped myself up on my elbow. "You just automatically assume that if something bad happened, it must be Mom's fault."

"No," Allison snapped back. "You just automatically assume Mom is as perfect as you are, so *nothing* could ever be her fault."

I pulled my pillow over my face and breathed in the

slightly sweaty smell of it. There was no reason to have this argument for the billionth time in the middle of the night. I heard my door swish open. I figured Allison was heading back to her room, or maybe to go wake up poor Phoebe and fill her with the worry Allison was clearly incapable of keeping to herself. Just as I lifted the pillow off my head to warn her to leave Phoebe alone, Allison's face loomed beside mine again.

"Yikes." I gasped.

"But think about this," Allison whispered. "If she's so innocent, why is Mom burning her papers in the fireplace at one in the morning?"

I sat up. Allison's face was all blotchy. I asked if she was sure and, her eyes open wide and scared, Allison slowly nodded.

My mouth was suddenly dry. I licked my parched lips with my sandpaper tongue. Trying to calm my pounding pulse, I breathed in through my nose and smelled it: the unmistakable nondream smell of a fire.

"She's burning papers?" I whispered.

"Yeah."

"You're sure? Because if there's just a fire we should—"

"I'm sure," Allison whispered. "I was watching. She's pulling them out of a binder and crumpling them and putting them in the fire."

I threw my covers off and followed my sister out of my

room. We tiptoed down the front stairs, skipping the fifth and seventh steps (the squeakers) and pressing close to the banister so we wouldn't bump the pictures on the wall. We could hear the crackling of the fire and my father's worried whispers.

"Claire, please," he was whispering.

We missed her next words because papers were being crumpled, but then heard her whisper fiercely, "my own private notes, my own private thoughts"—*crumple crumple*—"no right to"—*crumple crumple burn burn burn*.

"Indictable," he whispered back.

I wanted to get a look. If my mother was burning her papers, papers that were important in a legal case, and she wasn't supposed to, she could end up in jail. Her lawyer was a business lawyer; she had told me that—she had explained it to me very clearly, privately, not to my sisters but to me, because I am the oldest, the one she can count on, the one she knows would worry and project forward with *what if, what if, what if*. So she was very clear to me that this sphere of a man was a business lawyer; she was retaining him (*retaining*, that was the word she used, as if he was something she was keeping around like on a leash, just in case without really wanting to, almost accidentally, retaining him like retaining water) to handle issues of her severance pay, the terms of her leaving the company, how they'd word her letters of recommendation and something about a noncompete clause. I didn't follow all of what she was saying but I pretended to, because I wanted her to be able to talk to me in her fast-word shorthand, to trust me—and the important thing was that this Weeble of a lawyer was there to negotiate contracts for her, not to protect her from jail. She hadn't done anything wrong.

She was blameless.

Allison was blaming her but Allison was always blaming her. If Allison didn't get her homework done it was Mom's fault; if Allison overslept or got a zit it was Mom's fault.

But of course, in fact, it was not Mom's fault—neither Allison's zit nor the need for a lawyer. Obviously.

I moved down another step. It was June, late June, a heat wave, and after one in the morning. If there was a good reason for my parents to be making a fire in the family room, I was having trouble coming up with it. I turned to look at Allison, to signal her to be very quiet, and, slightly off balance, knocked with my left shoulder into an etching they'd recently bought by some old Dutch artist who wasn't Rembrandt, but almost.

Allison and I both froze.

Mom and Dad stopped moving behind the wall. "What was that?" my mother whispered, and her normally absolute voice sounded trembly.

Allison tugged my T-shirt at the shoulder, pulling me urgently upstairs.

"I'll see," Dad said. His footsteps started toward us.

I couldn't move.

Allison tugged again. Her face was intense and urging: *Come! Hurry! Now!* I couldn't remember how to make my muscles obey my brain.

If I stayed they'd find me there; they'd know I knew. It would all be out in the open. How awful. But . . . honesty, I thought. The best policy. Oh, great. Clichés, just the weapon I needed.

Something clicked in my nervous system. I dashed up behind Allison and didn't look back. At the top of the stairs we split—she went left, to her room; I went right to mine. I dove feet-first into my bed and slid quickly down under the blankets, between the cool three-hundred-thread-count organic white cotton sheets. I snuggled my head down into the well of my still-dented pillow and pretended to sleep, sure my telltale heart would give me away if my father had followed us up the stairs.

The next thing I knew, the sun was coming through my window.

I brushed my teeth carefully, concentrating on my morning routine, washing, moisturizing, smoothing my ponytail, choosing soft white socks and my camp shirt.

In the kitchen, watching our moody toaster work on a whole-wheat English muffin for us to share, Mom teased me about having passed out so early because I was worn out from anticipation of being responsible for so many kids.

I fake-smiled, like a twitch, and agreed, "Yes, it is defi-nitely exhausting."

Not wanting to meet her eyes, I watched the toaster, too. Mom sighed. Together we saw our English-muffin-to-share suddenly ignite inside our crazy toaster. As Mom tried to douse the flames, I tried not to breathe in the scent of burning.

Today was the first day with campers.

I was having trouble concentrating. I don't think I was a great role model. Jelly glanced over at me, concerned, a couple of times, but mostly she laughed more than usual, cracking up at everything Adriana said. They were having a lot of fun.

The two of them led our campers right into the pool, and together they all splashed around like a bunch of happy ducks. Only one sullen camper refused to go in, and since I was in no mood to be a happy duck myself, I made a big deal of being willing to sit with him. His name was Ramon, and he was one of the littlest of our campers. He sat still and silent on the bench, his bright towel draped over his narrow shoulders, so serious and thoughtful, his tangled black hair obscuring his dark eyes.

My first few attempts at conversation went nowhere. I

didn't honestly care. I leaned back against the chain-link fence and was trying not to think about my white room or my mother burning papers when Ramon announced, "I have no gills."

"True," I said, without opening my eyes.

"So I can't breathe the oxygen from the water."

"You don't have to," I mumbled. "You can breathe air, because you'll just float."

"How do *you* know?" he demanded.

"You're buoyant," I mumbled. I was so not up to being a role model right then.

"Not very," Ramon said sadly, and hunched over more. "I'm bad at throwing and I don't care about cars and I am not rough-and-tumble at all."

"So?"

"That's what boys are supposed to be!"

"Not boyish," I said quietly. "Buoyant."

He looked interested, and skeptical. I explained the principles of buoyancy and why he would float, and then that boys can still be boyish even without punching or being rough at all.

He listened intensely to everything I told him, then said, "Okay, I will swim tomorrow. I have to think about this for a while first."

I felt so tender toward him in that moment, I put my arm around him and he rested, heart pounding, his head against my chest.

I slumped into Jelly's car when it was time to go home. "You stressed about family stuff or your piano lesson or what?" she asked.

"All of life is stress," I said.

"You sound like me," Jelly pointed out.

"Someone has to," I mumbled, but I wasn't actually annoyed at her—I wasn't actually annoyed at anybody; I was just in a funk that needed to be overcome—so I turned on the rap music and pretended to happily seat-dance along. Sometimes faking is the fastest route to becoming.

I was still fake-happy at my piano lesson, trying to be, as Phoebe's stupid magazines admonish, lighthearted and fun to be with—because that's what guys like.

My fingers could not get their act together at all. Oliver touched them lightly. "Wait," he said. "Think first: What is this piece about?"

I hung my head, chastised. "I don't know."

"Good," he said. "Excellent place to begin. Scary, maybe, but if you're brave enough to admit not knowing, you open yourself up to what might be. Does that make sense to you?"

"Yes," I whispered.

"What do you feel when you hear it in your mind? What do you think?"

My mind was blank, so I just sat there, a tense lump of failure beside him.

"You okay?" Oliver asked me, in that rumbling baritone voice of his.

"Fine!" I smiled, or at least showed my shiny bleached
teeth. Urgh, what a dork. "Anyway, though, this is my last
lesson."

"Oh?" he asked.

I shrugged, all casual, as if I wasn't admitting for the
first time, "Money issues, you know."

He didn't say anything. I was staring at my fingers,
splayed uselessly across the keys. *Make a joke, make light of
it, pass it off,* I was commanding myself, but my normally
obedient self was stiffly rebelling. I swallowed, or tried.
I forced my mouth back into an imitation smile, and my
eyes up toward his. He wasn't making a *whatever, no big
deal* face, or turning away politely, embarrassed. He didn't
even look curious, hungry for the gossip, like most of the
people who live in this town absolutely would be. He just
sat still on the bench beside me, staring into my eyes.

Just what I needed. Full-body sweat. Did he have to
have such piercingly intelligent eyes, if he was going to be
too old for me and yet sit right beside me all smelling like
cilantro, and his black hair standing up so cute in back like
that? I mean, really.

"So," I started, desperate to not cry like the baby I
didn't want him to think I was. "Anyway."

He lifted his big, graceful hand from his lap and placed
it on my shoulder. It took all of my concentration to remain

conscious and still. I had my hair in a ponytail and a tank top on. I felt two of his fingertips on the skin of my neck, down where my neck curved toward my shoulder. His fingers, so warm, melted something inside me. I could feel it radiating moltenly from the points where his fingers touched my skin, down, down.

I didn't want to budge.

I'm not sure if I initiated the movement or he did with the pressure of those fingers, but I tilted toward him, slowly, until my head was against his shoulder.

His shirt was soft, the kind of cool silkiness a T-shirt acquires when it's been washed hundreds of times. I could feel his chest rising and falling beneath my cheek.

"You okay?" he asked, his voice just a whisper or less.

I intended to say yes. It came out instead as, "No."

I felt his arm tighten around me.

My sisters' voices on the stairs wrenched us apart. I couldn't look at him. I didn't want to look into his face and see clearly that he was comforting a little girl the way I had comforted little Ramon a few hours earlier.

The parallels were too hideous.

The idea of Oliver loving me like I had been loving toward Ramon shot me off the bench toward the living room door.

"So, thanks," I said quickly. "Sorry about the . . . lack of notice, or whatever. Hope it doesn't mess you up, or—"

"No worries," Oliver replied. "I just . . . Quinn. If you want to talk . . ."

"I'm not a baby!" I couldn't look at him. "I'm fine. Okay?"

I left without saying good-bye or walking him to the door. I ran up the stairs. He was the first person other than Jelly—oh, well, and Adriana—I had told we were in financial trouble; Mom had asked us to keep family business in the family, which meant secret. *Don't tell anybody.* I broke her trust, broke my word, traded my reliability for an embrace. And a lopsided embrace at that.

And also for what, in the case of Adriana? To seem cool and casual, to try out saying it? It was bad enough to have told Jelly. Why tell Adriana, whom I don't even know, and Oliver, whom I love in an embarrassing little-schoolgirl-crush kind of way, which I am much too old to continue indulging when he is all brilliant and perfect and off at college and having probably dozens of girlfriends, while I sit home in my little-girl world imagining whether I could ever be good enough, brilliant and beautiful and perfect enough, to make him really notice me? Ew!

Could I please finally accept that he is just way, way out of my league, that I will never be worthy of the kind of love I have to stop wanting from him?

I slammed my door and flopped down on my bed, waiting for tears that didn't come. *Big mouth*, I berated myself. I'd made such a big deal to my sisters about keeping Mom's privacy and now I'd sold it out for a cheap, one-sided, nonthrilling thrill.

Why?

Just for attention?

To get him, and them, to like me? For pity?

That was just too pathetic to contemplate.

Since I wasn't crying, I knelt to peek out my window, to watch Oliver leave. He didn't turn back to look at me.

I took it, as always, as a sign, proof that he felt, could feel, nothing for me.

But that night was the first time he texted me:

I know you're not a baby.

6

I DIDN'T TEXT BACK, not right away, and I didn't call him.

The next afternoon, instead of the romantic tryst I was forcing myself not to imagine, I failed my driver's test.

I had never failed a test before in my life. I'd gotten 100 percent on my permit test seven months earlier; the lady at the DMV couldn't believe it. She said she'd never seen a perfect score before, in twelve years of working at the Department of Motor Vehicles. She called a colleague over to see it. The guy, who looked like he'd never said no to a Twinkie, asked me, mockingly, if I'd studied for the test.

"Yes," I admitted, thinking, *Did I study? It was a test.*

I don't always get a perfect score on every test, obviously, but when I get something wrong it tortures me. Teachers held me up as an example starting in kindergarten, but, really, it isn't that I'm so brilliant the answers come easily to me or so diligent I would never shirk a responsibility as much as I am neurotic, and the pain of red Xs on my paper is so much worse than the pleasure (if there is pleasure in it) of not studying, there's barely a choice. Did I study? It was a test. Of course I studied.

Mom drove me to the driving test.

Dad used to drive us everywhere, do the stuff with us that most people's mothers did, make the little decisions that had to be handled every day, especially since Mom's work got so intense a few years ago. Allison was resentful of Mom's business busyness, but not me—I liked it that she was the money of our family, that the world took her so seriously and rewarded her so richly (literally) for her hard work and brilliance at what she did.

Huh. Maybe it was just the weirdness of having her drive me to my driving test, her awkwardness and deeply unhelpful attempts to bond (probe) when I was trying to focus, her disorienting new need to get in my head that screwed me up at that vital moment.

Or maybe I was feeling slightly, well, disappointed in her, judging her harshly—which was so unfair and just plain incorrect that it completely threw me off my game.

Or maybe I actually suck at driving, despite my sisters' oft-repeated belief that I am excellent at it in their impatience to have me drive them everywhere. Maybe they are just fooled about that, too.

Whatever the cause of my distraction or lack of talent during the test, though, and whatever the mitigating circumstances—like the squirrel that truly did, whether Driving Inspector Man saw it or not, run in front of the car as I was attempting the three-point turn—it is not really under dispute whether or not I smashed into that police car.

I mean, the siren went off.

Or, rather, went on.

And on and on and on.

Nobody was injured or anything. It was a small dent. I am not trying to make excuses for myself. I agree that the driving instructor was well within his rights to fail me. Though I will admit the thought crossed my mind that this is some impressive job for an adult to have—did this dude dream when he was seventeen of someday becoming the judge and jury on whether kids who were nervous and doing their best to block out the rest of their stressful lives and focus on making three-point turns (which never in my life have I witnessed a driver actually making) without committing a small mistake like, *Whoops that is actually still in reverse!*, should be given a second chance after their profuse and, I should add, immediately accepted apologies to the cops whose car they smashed?

But what I said aloud was, "Of course, I understand. I hope your neck feels better soon."

Then I slipped quietly into the passenger seat of my mother's car and waited for her to drive away.

Instead, she turned to me, her hand loose on the

gearshift of her Porsche. "What happened?" she asked, not unsympathetically.

I shrugged.

"Well, of course you passed."

"I didn't," I told her. "Can we go?"

"You are so hard on yourself," Mom said. "I'm sure you did much better than you think you did."

"Uh, no."

"Tell me what happened," she cajoled, her voice smooth steel like always, despite her lack of cajoling practice. "It's probably like that time you thought you'd failed your presentation in seventh grade because you hesitated for a second, and said, horror of horrors, 'Excuse me,' before you continued. Do you remember? And you got an A-plus on that, if I remember correctly."

She did not remember correctly. I got an A. I gritted my teeth. She was always bringing up that story.

"Come on, Quinn, what happ—"

"I smashed into a police car," I said.

She blinked twice. "By smashed, do you mean—"

"Did you hear the siren?"

She clapped her hand over her mouth. "That was you?"

I tilted my head and half smiled. "Yeah."

"No!"

I thought: *We can't all be as perfect as you, Mom.*

I said: nothing.

"A cop car?" She was actually starting to laugh. "Seriously, Quinn? You crashed into a cop car on your driving test?"

"Can we go?" I asked again, then added, "Please?"

Mom turned the key in the ignition. "I can't believe . . . Was anybody hurt?"

"No," I said. "Well, Driving Inspector Man was grumbling about his neck, but—"

"Were they in pursuit of criminals, at least? And cut you off? It was probably their fault," she tried, racing through a yellow light.

"They were drinking sodas, parked," I admitted.

"No!" Tears were streaming down Mom's cheeks, she was laughing so hard.

"Air bags pop out at like the least provocation, don't they?" I asked.

"Oh, Quinn!" She pulled into a gas station and yanked up the emergency brake in front of the pump. "Did they really?"

I shrugged. "Not in Driving Inspector Man's car. Just the cruiser."

Mom was laughing so hard she banged her head down on the wheel, which beeped, causing everybody to look at us. Awesome, just what I needed.

"You need help, ma'am?" a guy at the other pump asked, checking my mother out. It would be awkward if I weren't completely used to such things.

She waved her hand dismissively. "No, no, thanks. We're fine."

She flung open her door and grabbed her purse. I sank down in my seat, feeling like the failure I absolutely was at that moment. Her knock on my door startled me.

"See if you can find any change," she asked me.

"What? Where?" I asked.

"Below the seat," she said. "Glove compartment?"

I dug down, trying not to think beyond the project at hand. After excavations with both hands, I came up with a pen, two dollar bills, eighty-seven cents, and a corner of a map showing far northeast Maine. And dirt under my short fingernails. I sorted the money out and handed it to Mom. "I have a ten," I told her, grabbing for my bag.

"No, this'll do us," she said, and strode across the gas place toward the convenience store/paying place like a lady in a perfume commercial.

She had never paid cash for gas before, to say nothing about scrounging for change to buy it.

Scrounging for change in her Porsche.

She strode back out and pumped the gas expertly into the car. I had never witnessed either of my parents getting less than a full tank of gas before.

By the time she got back into the driver's seat, all my annoyance at her for distracting me from my driver's test with her questions on the way there about whether I had any crushes and how was camp going and was I okay with taking a breather from piano lessons for the summer—all that had evaporated. Questions tumbled through my mind: What was going to happen to our family? Were we really going to have to move? To where? Could she even get a new mortgage? We weren't going to be homeless, were we? And if we were, where was she going to park her Porsche? I don't know if they have secure garages at homeless shelters. Why had she needed to burn her papers? Why had she really gotten fired?

But I didn't ask anything.

I watched her face.

Her beautiful face, fierce eyes that could turn in a fraction of a second from laughing Caribbean blue to cold hard steel; perfect, pert nose; unlined, unblemished skin . . .

For the first time I noticed there were lines on her forehead. Two parallel lines shooting up from the sides of her nose, like railroad tracks splitting her forehead. Her lips were chapped; a fleck of skin tipped off the center of the bottom lip, ready to dive toward her chin but teetering on the edge of her smudged gloss. The semicircles under her eyes were slightly poochy, and shadowy, too.

My stomach clenched.

She forced another giggle, but it was not spontaneous anymore. "You have to tell Daddy about that. He will die laughing!"

That didn't seem like a consummation devoutly to be wished, at least not in the short run, but I forced a smile, too, and promised to trot out my failure for the amusement (hopefully not terminal) of my father, and then also my sisters. Sure, why not. If I couldn't bring home the achievement, the certificate, the medal, I may as well perform the story of my failure for them all, I selfishly, self-pityingly thought.

Mom was right. They all loved the story that night at dinner. Nobody actually died, but all of them, at various points, did gasp for air. Especially Daddy. He was banging the table, cracking up. I admit I embellished the story in a few places, like the Coca-Cola stains on the front of the skinnier cop's pants. It's hard to sort out what actually happened, because now I remember it as I told it, and more than that, I remember how delighted they seemed with my story.

Even in flunking, I could bring joy to my parents.

7

THE NEXT MORNING ALLISON was in the kitchen when I got down. I knew better than to ask what was going on, or why she was awake. I went straight to the fridge to get the milk for cereal. There was barely a drop in the whole container.

Without turning to her, I asked, "Did you drink all the milk?"

"You just assume it was me," Allison responded.

I put the milk back in. Dad would want the dribble that was left for his tea. I chose a plum from the fruit drawer and shut the fridge.

Allison's crazy cell phone was freaking out on the counter in front of her. She was staring right down at it, her head tepeed on her hands, not answering it.

A normal phone surrenders after a while and sends the caller to voice mail, but not Allison's, apparently. It just kept right on going, playing an ABBA tune I knew I'd be condemned to hum the rest of the day.

"Phone," I said.

"You think?" Allison said.

"Who are you ignoring?"

"Tyler."

"Your boyfriend calls you at eight in the morning and you—"

"He's not my boyfriend."

"Oh," I said. News to me. "Okay."

The phone stopped playing ABBA. The silence was loud.

I wasn't sure if I should comfort Allison, and if so, how to go about it. I've known her since she was born, but still. Allison is a porcupine.

Before I could choose my move, her phone started having a seizure.

"I broke up with him last night," Allison explained.

"*You* broke up with *him*?"

"Thanks," she said. "Nice."

"I didn't mean . . ." But of course I did. Busted. Change the subject: "That him again?"

She looked at me like I was an idiot. "No, the mailman."

Tyler Moss was the widely acknowledged hottest guy in my grade. He went out with a senior at the beginning of tenth grade, and then fooled around with basically every gorgeous girl in the school, and then fell in love with my sister. I am not particularly looped into the gossip chains, but even I knew everybody was saying Tyler Moss was totally whipped over Allison. They were the IT couple of the end of the school year.

He was the first guy Allison ever went out with.

And she broke up with him? I couldn't believe it. I am a big believer in female power and the desirability of offbeat, intense, different-drummer girls. I totally thought Tyler was lucky and smart to fall for Allison, but, well, nobody would break up with Tyler Moss.

I am also serious about not prying. It was none of my business what happened between them.

"What happened?" I asked her accidentally.

She rolled her eyes. "Nothing."

"Did he do something to you?" Allison had never even kissed a boy before, and Tyler Moss was not exactly known for his prudery. "I'll kill him."

Allison burst out laughing. "What happened to my sister, Gandhi reincarnated?"

"I'll chop off his private parts and staple them to his butt," I vowed, shocking us both.

"Quinn!" Phoebe said from the doorway.

"Who goes from Zen master straight to Mafia enforcer without passing Go?" Allison asked, smiling a bit in spite of herself.

"Seriously," Phoebe agreed. "Holy Quinn."

They were both looking at me with renewed respect. I

shook my head. "I didn't—"

"So who's getting stapled?" Phoebe asked, helping herself to a smoothie from the fridge.

"Ty," Allison said. "It just wasn't working out."

Phoebe's face drooped in sympathy. She spread her arms and gathered Allison into them. "Oh, Al," she murmured.

I stood there like a stranger waiting for a train.

Allison's phone honked twice. We all looked at it. Allison's eyebrows crunched in the center of her face. She shrugged and picked up the phone. After she said hello she just sat there on a stool, listening, so Phoebe and I turned away to give her some privacy, and also to look toward where Mom's high heels were clacking across the foyer toward us.

"The warranty on my vehicle may be expiring," Allison explained, hanging up as Mom came into the kitchen.

"What vehicle?" Mom asked, pouring herself a cup of coffee from the pot on the counter.

"Exactly," Allison said.

"Ew." Mom swallowed hard. "Your father makes the worst coffee. Where is he?"

"Is everybody always up this early?" Allison asked.

"Can I go over to Luke's?" Phoebe asked. "And can I stay for dinner, because—"

"Daddy and I may be out late; we have . . ." Mom checked her watch as she poured the mugful of coffee down the drain. "He didn't go out for a run, did he?"

"I'm going back to bed," Allison announced, sliding off the stool, phone in hand. "This whole *morning* thing sucks."

Jelly beeped in the driveway for me. I said good-bye and stepped forward to kiss Mom on the cheek, but she bent her head at the same instant, checking her watch, so I just kind of jolted past her.

"We have a meeting with the lawyers in forty minutes," she said. "Where is . . ."

Dad flumped down the back stairs at that moment. We all stopped short and watched him walk his long-legged, loose-limbed amble into the kitchen, because instead of his usual summer look (raggedy khaki shorts, loose T-shirt, battered old Keds) he had on a dark suit, crisp white shirt, and blue tie. His hair was even gelled back. He looked like the movie star who would play Dad in a big-budget film.

"Who the hell are you?" Allison muttered.

Phoebe was looking back and forth between Mom and Dad, so I turned to see Mom's expression, too. She was half smirking, but her eyes were soft, and her head was shaking slowly. She lifted her arms as he approached her, and as I left, they were embracing in the kitchen. Allison didn't realize I could see her spying on them around the corner, partway up the back stairs.

I think it was the romance between them that infected my brain. That's the excuse I made to myself anyway. I

55

was slumped in the front seat of Jelly's car, my stuff in my bag on my lap, my head tapping Morse-code messages of loneliness onto the window, as Jelly alternately rocked out (when she remembered a word or two of the song playing) and talked about Adriana and the parties we'd go to with her.

Without letting myself think it through, I yanked my phone out of my bag and texted Oliver.

It was nothing huge or horribly embarrassing. Just, *Hi.* I hit SEND before I could add to it, or subtract.

"Who'd you text?" Jelly asked between songs.

I shrugged. "Oliver."

"Shut *up*!"

"He texted me the other night, so—"

"He babysat you," Jelly reminded me for the billionth time.

"He babysat Phoebe," I argued.

"While you were there," she pointed out. "And he got paid."

"A hundred years ago."

"I just don't want you to get hurt," Jelly said tenderly. "You know that."

"Yeah," I said. "I do."

I held my phone the rest of the way to camp, willing it to beep with a reply message. In fact I held it most of the day, so much so that Adriana asked me if I was waiting for my boyfriend to text me.

"No," Jelly said. "Her piano teacher."

"Your piano teacher?" Adriana asked, as if it were my SAT tutor or, ew, my driving test man.

"He's hot," Jelly quickly explained. "And in college."

"Oh," Adriana said, with renewed interest. "I get it. Practice, practice, practice . . ."

"It's not like that," I said. When she raised one perfectly arched eyebrow, I clarified, "At least, it's not . . . for him."

"I get it," she said. "He thinks you're just a high school girl."

"Yeah," I said. "Possibly because I am."

"That whole reality thing," Jelly agreed.

"Screw reality; I have a better idea," Adriana said. We were leading the campers down the hill to the arts-and-crafts shack. Jelly and I had to wait to hear the better idea until all the campers had been seated at benches and given lanyard strings. While the arts-and-crafts counselors got them going on that, Jelly, Adriana, and I went out to sit on the steps of the cabin.

"There's this guy," Adriana said. "I think you'd really like him, Quinn. His name is Mason. He's sick hot."

"How about me?" Jelly asked. "I need somebody sick hot, too."

"No fears," Adriana said. "Mason's best friend is this guy JD. He's mad wild."

"Perfect," Jelly said, convinced. "Mad wild. I like that."

"I don't think Mason sounds like my type," I protested. "And this JD . . ."

"He's anybody's type," Adriana insisted. "Tell you what: you guys will come over to my house Saturday. I'm having a few people over and you'll see if you like them. They're friends of my boyfriend *du semaine*, Giovanni. Who is so hot it's probably illegal. No more mooning over Piano Man, though, right? Summer is for fun."

"Exactly," Jelly said. "Well, fun and padding the résumés." Jelly tilted her head toward our campers, who were already streaming out the arts-and-crafts door.

"Come on, you rungs on our résumés," Adriana said. "Who rules?"

"Hawks!" they all shouted, all except Ramon, who slipped his cool little hand into mine as we walked back up the hill.

The Saturday night fix-up plan was revisited a few times over the course of the day. I gave up arguing. I just shrugged and went along with the idea, knowing (well, thinking I knew) that nothing would ever come of it.

It's not that I think I suck, or am ugly, or that I am socially awkward to the point of should-look-into-a-convent. The opposite, almost. I can pass. I know I can. The pretty girls, the fashionable, socially buzzy girls, are and have always been very nice to me. Like Adriana, they tend to be, in my experience and counter to the stereotype of obnoxious "popular" girls, very inclusive. And I like them; I do—they are generally a lot more fun in some ways than my brainy friends other than (well, sometimes including) Jelly: the smart, sardonic, depressed and depressing, poetry-quoting, black-wearing, disaffected, self-consciously outsiderish nerd friends. The social girls are generally happier, for one thing, and up for a good time. The problem is, I get a headache when I spend too much time with them. It's the accents, the whine in their voices, the entitled attitude, the grabbing one another's arms and whispering in one another's ears, the in-crowd behavior that makes me feel sleepy first and then itchy.

When I am with the nihilistic geniuses I long for pastels and smiley faces. When I am with the materialistic supersocialites I fall into a pit of self-loathing and minor chords.

Hard to believe I am the easy kid in my family. I am such a pain in the ass. Nobody usually knows that, though. I am the ultimate con girl. In American Culture AP this past year, we learned about the racial issue of "passing"—there was a thing, historically, that if you were an African American who had lighter skin, you could supposedly "pass" for white and therefore were likely to attain a higher rank in society. Pretty awful, when you think about the implications of that. In my school and my life, it isn't so much a matter of race or ethnic background. There's a money element, definitely, though how much impact that has I guess I will find out in the coming year, when we have none, or much less, anyway. But even more than money, and way more than skin color, I think, is social grace, or interest, maybe. Like, if you know how to whisper and laugh and say the right thing to a particular crowd, that's who you hang with, even if that's not who you really are.

I could pass for anything.

Well, not a jock. But I could pass for cool and hyper-social, or brainy, or even theater geek and, of course, band freak.

People usually bought what I put on display.

I had always thought of it as a skill, something good— I didn't confine myself to one group. Also it was like a secret. I was a spy, able to pass undetected in any guise I chose, and nobody would know the real me.

Except Oliver. It has always felt like he could see right through, like he wasn't fooled, though he was maybe amused. It's that, I think, that makes him so irresistible to me. Not just how his butt looks in jeans, no matter what my crass sisters say, too loudly, as he leaves our house after lessons. It's just that it feels like he sees who I really am when he looks in my eyes.

Or maybe that is all just my fantasy. My horribly deluded fantasy, and something I have to move on from.

Because he didn't respond to my text. My phone stayed limp and lifeless as a sandwich in my hand all the sweaty day.

Nobody even wanted to let me know my nonexistent warranty was about to expire.

"Screw him," Jelly said when she caught me checking

it on the drive home. "Not literally, of course. Excelsior. Bigger and better and sicker and wilder guys await us. Right?"

"Right," I agreed.

"There's wildness in us," she insisted, making all the windows go down at once. "Before the grind of junior year starts, we have to let our crazy wildness *out!*"

So that, plus the romance of my parents and the twittering of Adriana and Jelly and their escalating plans for fun this summer with the mad-sick-wild, etc., Mason and JD, and the lack of response from Oliver and maybe even the humid heat had sent me into a bit of a crazed and desperate funk even before I got home to find the house echoingly empty until the doorbell rang.

None of that is sufficient excuse, I am aware, for what happened. I'm just saying they are all pieces of the reason.

8

I HAD TO INTERRUPT MY PARENTS at the lawyer's office. No way was I letting those three bulky men in the door without finding out if I was even supposed to, or allowed to.

Dad answered Mom's cell.

He answered all my questions, sometimes saying, "Hold on," to confer with Mom and the lawyer. I had to read him the document handed to me by the short guy with the stubble darkening his cheeks. All three of them stared at me with arms crossed but not objecting as I listened to murmurs of discussion through the phone. The men seemed kind, patient, and way out of proportion for our mudroom, which had until that moment been plenty big.

"Okay," I told Dad, but then added, "You sure?"

"Yeah," he said. "Gotta go."

His voice cracked.

I closed my phone and turned to the men. "Okay."

"Can you show us where the piano is?"

I led them through the kitchen and around through the foyer to the living room. I pointed at the piano, though at that point it was probably obvious to them where the piano was.

There was some muttering and measuring, and a bit of difficulty with unjamming the second double front door, which I had actually never seen open before. It looked unseemly, embarrassing to have such a gaping opening to our house, like a girl wearing a skirt with her knees spread.

I leaned against the living room wall while they worked, then went and sat at a stool in the kitchen. It occurred to me I should probably be overseeing what they were doing, making sure they weren't denting the walls or stealing the coasters, but I couldn't rouse myself to give a crap, and honestly I didn't really want to watch them removing the piano.

When the piano was out, presumably in the truck, the head guy brought me a paper to sign. "We just need your autograph," he said jovially, but his squinty eyes showed he knew this was awkward. He shrugged with one shoulder as I placed the crinkled papers on the granite counter to sign on the line.

I closed the double doors behind them.

I tried to get up the courage to go into the living room and see it all empty and stripped, but I just couldn't. Instead I opened both the double doors again.

I stood there and looked out at the front yard for a while.

Then I turned around and forced myself to go to the living room.

There were deep indents in the carpet where the piano feet had been. Above them was way too much air. And silence.

When it hit me that the music was gone, that we would go to sleep that night without hearing "Summertime," listening only to the thudding of our own hearts, I sat down in the space where the piano wasn't and held my head in my hands. I waited for tears that didn't show and wished simultaneously for somebody to come home so we could deal together, and yet for nobody to come home because it wouldn't be fully real until somebody did, until I connected with somebody about it.

I heard a creak behind me but didn't look up, because only Phoebe walks that quietly, and a sudden wave of guilt had knocked me so sideways, I couldn't face her. Obviously it wasn't my fault that our piano had been repossessed, but I was the one who let them take it. I didn't stop them. I was supposed to be the one who made sure nothing bad happened. Three men came and took our piano; I let them—I signed a paper saying yes, take what was ours, our magnificent grand piano that I will never play again in my whole life.

That's when the tears came, and when the voice that said, "Hey," behind me was not Phoebe's.

Startled, I looked up.

It was Tyler Moss.

"Quinn," he said.

I rubbed at my eyes like a little kid, and sniffled. "Allison's not here."

"What happened?" he asked.

What happened.

"You kind of . . . It's a bad . . ."

He knelt in front of me. "Hey."

"They took our piano."

"Were you robbed? The big doors were wide-open. . . ."

I shook my head. "No," I said. "Worse."

"You okay?" he asked.

I swallowed and tried to smile. "Yeah."

He was staring into my eyes, so tender, his eyes the most intense blue I had ever seen. He mumbled some words of comfort that didn't comfort me at all.

And then, I don't know, I started crying again. He hugged me; I hugged him. He was comforting me, like a friend, like an old friend, even though in truth he was not my friend, not an old friend despite the fact that he was in my grade and until a few hours before that had been going out with my sister. But I was kneeling then, too, and he was holding me, right there on the rug where the piano wasn't, and then, though I had never kissed a boy before, I kissed him.

9

I STOPPED AS SOON AS I realized what I was doing.

Of course.

I really did.

Well, almost as soon.

What does that even mean, *as soon as I realized*? It's not like I completely didn't realize what I was doing. I wasn't a cabbage at the moment our lips met, obviously. My brain was functioning, though clearly not fully, and my body was following my brain's commands.

And then some.

But I was also thinking.

I was thinking many, many things all at once. One of which was, *Oh, my God.* Another of which was, *I am finally kissing somebody—hallelujah, I will not graduate from high school unkissed, and by the way, this boy I am kissing happens to be the hottest boy in my grade, hooray for me, and his lips are both soft and hard.* Another thought dashing across my brain was, *Mmmm.*

I may also have been thinking, on another track, *Kissing actually is a very lovely and enjoyable activity; now I see why so many songs are written about this wonderful thing; I must figure out how to do it again often.*

I just wasn't thinking, *Absolutely not. I cannot kiss my sister's boyfriend, or ex-boyfriend, if he really is ex.*

The main thing I was thinking about in those few seconds (honestly it was no more than four or possibly five seconds) while I was kissing Tyler Moss and forcing myself not to be thinking, *No!*, was what he had said, trying to comfort me, right before somehow our bodies were mashed up against each other down to the knees (we were kneeling) and up to the lips:

"It's just things."

Which, okay, obviously. On one level. And for goodness' sake, my nickname (not that I completely have a nickname, like at school, to put on my jacket if I were on a team, but from my dad) is Zen. It's not like I am all about things.

"It's just things"?

That's what he came up with to comfort me, when three burly men had just removed our grand piano from the living room and left me home to be the one who already knew, when everybody else came home to find the living room excavated?

I know it's just things, I was thinking.

I know we are so blessed that our family is alive and intact and able to weather whatever hits us. I know what the important stuff is and isn't, you dumb, stupid, condescending jock, with, okay, an amazingly hard body and the staring eyes. But still, you honestly don't have to give me a greeting-card rally lesson on values. I get it. I got it.

On the other hand (and yes, I had time to think all this as I was making out with him, and no, that doesn't mean it was an hour-long session or anything; I just think very fast), it is actually not just things that got taken away.

That piano was a gift from my mother to my father, for one thing. It has symbolic value—as a huge, shiny testament to their success and her love for him and his for her—how she gave it to him because he loves to play the piano and had dreams, unfulfilled and even unspoken beneath all his protestations of always wanting to be a kindergarten teacher, of being a concert pianist but realizing early on that he had neither the drive nor the talent to be that— my mom told me all that when she was looking secretly at the Steinway brochure for the perfect grand piano to buy for him, and maybe she thought I forgot or wasn't paying attention, but I was; I always am. She believed in him, was what it said, sitting there all large in the living room. And he adored her, it sang, every night when he played— he played for us, of course, and for himself—but mostly he played for her, love song after love song; even a silly song like "Does Your Chewing Gum Lose Its Flavor on the Bedpost Overnight?" was a love song, really, because we all knew (or at least I knew) he was singing on some level to get that smile out of her.

And not to be selfish, but hello, I have been taking piano lessons on that piano for four years. I play that thing every single day. They may as well have taken away my fingers.

Or my voice.

Just things?

They even took the bench where Mom sometimes sat next to Dad, or one of us did (usually Phoebe), and also where, for the past year, I sat every week for half an hour beside Oliver.

They took the damn bench.

Seriously, how much does a damn bench cost?

Just things. Right.

But sometimes things are more than just things.

So I pulled my mouth off Tyler Moss's mouth and opened my eyes.

We stared at each other for a second, maybe three. "Quinn . . ." he said.

I stood up. "You'd better get out of here," I told him, with my hand over my mouth.

"I didn't . . ." he said. "I'm sorry."

I shook my head.

Behind me, I heard him standing up.

"Quinn . . ."

"Don't tell Allison," I said, my back still to him. "Please."

"I won't," he said. "I came here to . . ."

"Just go," I said, and dashed up the stairs.

No doors closed behind him. I guess he went out the splayed double doors and left them like that.

I threw open my window, too, despite the blasting air-conditioning, and lay flat on my bed for, I don't know, hours. Forever. Trying not to think, not checking my phone or email because I certainly had forfeited any right to even hope for my own romantic anything. I pushed thoughts of Oliver and even (how did these sneak in there?) weird romantic images of this Mason person, whom I'd never met and would almost surely dislike, out of my festering head. I knew I deserved to be punished for what I had done, and that somehow, cosmically, I would get what I deserved. And I'd have no right to complain.

I always had this somewhat (okay, hugely) arrogant belief that, sure, I was extremely fortunate—materially, of course, but also in the family I got and the brains, the talents, even the actual unmagnified, perhaps puny talents I could honestly claim—blessed, really, any way you look at it. But that (here's the arrogant part, which I never fully articulated to myself until this second) I kind of in a way deserved all that. I was a good girl. I worked hard. I was responsible. I didn't smoke or drink or take drugs or curse or even stay up very late. I was honest with my parents and revised my work. I didn't gossip or wear tons of eyeliner. So why shouldn't I have good stuff? Why shouldn't I get the position at the camp I applied for, or straight As, win the piano competition, be selected "Best Girl" in my camp bunk? I earned it.

I had heard the phrase *the best and the brightest* lots of times in my life, and who wouldn't want to be that? I was willing to work for it, and when I was considered that, one of the best and the brightest, well, it wasn't unearned, right?

But someone who is "the best" or "the brightest" doesn't kiss her sister's boyfriend. Even if he is recently demoted to ex-boyfriend.

Even if it "just happened." An accident, a mistake. Everybody makes a mistake sometimes, right?

Do things really just happen, though? Or was there a little part of me that, seeing Tyler Moss there in front of me with those sizzling eyes and that intense body, the hottest boy in *my* grade, not my sister's grade, thought, *Well, why not* me? Forbidden, naughty—absolutely—but maybe for one freaking second of my life I could be naughty, grab the forbidden thing? Why does Allison always get to be the wild child? Maybe just this once it could be me?

And then, to feel him respond . . . Because, okay, fine, I started it, I initiated it, I admit that I caused the kiss, true—but he responded. He did. He was kissing me back. He didn't pull away, not instantly, anyway. He kissed me, too.

Oh, my God.

I did not *just do that!*

A girl who would do a thing like that was nobody I'd want to associate with.

Which caused a couple of problems. Like, logistically, for starters.

I heard my parents as they were coming up the walk toward home after their appointment with the lawyer. I rolled off my bed and looked at my unrecognizable self, in my unrecognizable room. My heart skittered inside my chest. I had to do something. What? I looked like Psycho Girl, the whites visible all around the irises in my eyes.

Mom's heels were clicking just as confidently as ever on the path. I dashed to my bed and peeked over the edge of my windowsill and heard her saying to Dad, loud and clear because she was confident nobody was listening (memo to parents: We are always listening), "No, I didn't burn my journal, because that would be spoliation of evidence."

To which he very ethically responded, "Oh, Claire."

"I'm just not the kind of person who'd do such a thing," she said.

And something in me snapped. I slammed my window closed, and too bad if it startled them or they realized they were not in a cone of silence to discuss their transgressions like they were junk mail.

Apparently they noticed the open double doors. I heard them down there, but when they called to me I just said, "I'm in my room."

I tried not to listen to them after that. I tried not to hear them discussing what was going to happen next, what was next to go, "mortgage . . . impossible . . . your mother . . . You spoke with her? . . . temporary . . . What can we do? . . . We'll be okay. . . ."

I put my iPod earbuds in and wrecked my hearing for a while by blasting Rachmaninoff's entire second piano concerto.

When my sisters came home, they discovered the lack of piano, too.

"On credit," I heard Mom explaining. "Loan . . . finance . . . terms . . . belt-tightening."

"But it's ours," I heard Allison protest.

"Does Quinn know?" Phoebe asked.

Murmur murmur, came the response. My excellent hearing apparently had been successfully dulled. I was glad.

I was called down for dinner. Dad had whipped up a pasta dish with cauliflower and smoked Gouda, which we all ate with fake smiles and polite conversation.

I could not look at Allison at all.

Afterward, when all the plates were cleared, while he was washing the dishes, Dad joked, "Well, I guess I could ask a couple guys to come over and help me haul the upright up from the basement."

"I doubt it would be worth it," Mom muttered, then turned to us. "Girls, this is not going to be easy. The piano is only the first thing to go. You need to prepare yourselves—we all need to prepare. . . ."

By instinct I reassured her: "Don't worry about us, Mom. We're fine. We'll be fine." But I couldn't, this time, look her in the eyes, either.

"I'm just saying," she continued, shutting me down without a thought, not noticing how pissed I was despite my reassurances to her. "It's not going to be easy. . . ."

"We're the Avery Women," Phoebe chimed in. "Nothing can intimidate us."

Dad splashed her with his soapy hands. "Not even dish soap?"

"Well, maybe dish soap," Phoebe responded.

Dad dried his hands on the dish towel and said, "Okay, then, let's face our demons, shall we?"

We followed him into the cavernous living room. We stood there silently for a little while, not knowing what to do or where to go. After a minute or so, Dad wrapped his arms around Mom and said, "While it lasted, it sure was grand."

She buried her head in his chest. He looked up at the ceiling, which is my trick, too, for not letting tears fall out.

This time, though, the trick didn't work for me.

Suddenly I was on the floor, gasping for air through my sobs. My sisters hugged me, or tried, both at the same time, but I shrugged them off. I didn't mean to be making a scene, and the last thing I could handle was their comfort.

Allison looked at me with sad eyes, and Phoebe whispered, "You loved that piano, huh, Quinn?"

Mom and Dad turned to stare at me, too, as I cracked apart all over the empty living room. They looked shocked. I'd never lost it like that before. "Quinn . . ." Mom and Dad both started at the same time.

I shook my head, held up my hand to stop anyone from coming to hug me. I'd had enough of that earlier in the day and didn't deserve—couldn't take—any more.

The caring in their faces literally made me gag, and then I had to struggle to catch my breath again. It hit me hard how much I hated that they all had this image of me: the gifted one, the pianist who voluntarily—no, let's face it, compulsively—practiced, who gave concerts and won awards, the one who actually could, with luck and work and dedication, become a professional piano player, an artist, a master.

Not true, probably, but still, it was what they thought. And I'd let them. I'd liked their thinking it, despite knowing I wasn't that good at all.

They were staring at me, my whole family, the people closest in the world to me, but what they were seeing was the Photoshop version of me, retouched and improved, untrue. They had no idea it wasn't real.

They all thought I was shattered by the loss of the piano, that my dashed dreams of myself and our family had to do with competing, winning, music, beauty, success.

They were wrong. That wasn't what I was mourning. Not even close.

"It's just things," I told them, and ran upstairs alone.

10

THE NEXT NIGHT WE WENT to the fireworks at the high school. Adriana invited Jelly and me to go to a party with her, but I explained we had a family tradition, and Jelly said she had the same. Adriana rolled her eyes and empathized and we said good-bye with promises about Saturday at Adriana's house and meeting JD and Mason, either one or both of whom had previously made out with Adriana. Jelly talked the whole way home from camp about how cool it would be to feel so casual about having made out with this guy and that and then, "No big deal, we can just stay friends." Wouldn't that be awesome? "We should totally cultivate that," she suggested. I had to open my window for some air.

"Maybe if you made out with Mason, you'd stop obsessing about what's-his-name," she said.

I jolted toward her. "Who? Why do you think I am obsessed with somebody?"

"Oliver," she said meekly. "Who you have been obsessed with since, I don't know, ever. Jeez, Quinn. What?"

"Nothing. I'm just . . . in a weird mood," I said. "Sorry."

"Perpetual bad mood, Q. Seriously, lately. It's July, dude. We are going to get kissed this summer, and get wild, shed our outer dorkiness. But you have to chill."

"I will."

"Okay," she said. "Could you hurry, though? Because Saturday is coming up."

"I know. But, Jelly, honestly, I am not obsessed with Oliver."

"Yeah, right. Uh-huh. And did you know 'gullible' is written on the ceiling of my car?"

"Ha, ha, ha."

"No," she said. "Actually, it is." She was bursting with laughter. "It is, Quinn."

"Jelly, that's like a fourth-grade joke. Shedding our outer dorkiness?"

"Is it?" She looked deflated. "I still think it's funny." She pointed up.

I rolled my eyes and looked. There, in black Sharpie, in Jelly's beautifully perfect, neat handwriting, was the word *gullible* written small and dark against the tan felt.

I had to laugh. "Okay, I think that's funny, too. I can't believe you did that!"

"It's the worst thing I ever did. How sad is that? I'm in,

like, living torment that my dad will see it and freak out. He will so take the car away. And yet, can I say I am loving the buzz of having done it?"

I laughed again. "Wish I didn't get exactly what you mean."

She shrugged, pulling into my driveway. "My worst rebellion is nerdy, though."

"Totally nerdy." I grabbed my bag and got out. "But so darn funny."

"Let's talk tonight about what to wear to Adriana's tomorrow," she yelled on her way down my driveway.

I waved and nodded, though I fully intended to find an excuse not to go when the time came. I'd been to that kind of party before, without Jelly, who'd never been invited until now. I'd explained to her, after each, that they were boring: The people who got drunk made fools of themselves and the rest of us pretended to look for somebody so we wouldn't seem as bored as we actually were, and then eleven o'clock finally arrived and a person could leave with only shrugs and groans about unfair, though completely made-up, curfews (because my parents had never given me one, but nobody needed to know that) and not be thought a loser. Jelly was too psyched, though. She was out from behind the stacks in the library and determined to find all the glamour she imagined at Adriana's house, with a bunch of horny, drunk boys casting their eyes quickly over and past us, for sure.

Inside, Gosia was standing beside all her stuff, hugging each of us good-bye. Phoebe had made her a card, and Allison gave her a string bracelet she'd made. They were both crying, and Gosia was trying not to. She'd never be in our house again. She promised to call and check on us, and made us promise to email her all the time. "You're my girls; you always will be," she said, starting another round of hugs.

I just kept looking at the ceiling, and after she walked out the door, I went upstairs.

After a few hours of hiding in my white room, I piled into the car with my family and headed for the summer-deserted high school. The five of us sat on a big sheet like we used to when we were little, but none of us could get too excited about the fireworks. Dad said "ooh" and "ahh," especially at the grand finale, but to me it just seemed like a loud, profligate waste of money and time. The economy is in the toilet but we can blow up minibombs in the sky: Your tax dollars at work! When meanwhile some of my campers sometimes had nothing but ketchup and crackers for dinner. That's what skinny little Ramon had told me he'd had for dinner the night before, anyway, and it made my stomach clench. It was hard to get enthusiastic about the pops and whirs with that in mind, you know? Or maybe I was just feeling sour and self-righteous.

Maybe I was sad about Gosia leaving, and about not crying when she pulled away, as Allison and Phoebe had.

Maybe I just didn't feel like sitting on a blanket with my family.

Independence Day, I kept thinking. *So let's blow some stuff up. Woo-hoo. Then get some ice cream and straggle home.*

Because what says independence more than pointless destruction?

I smiled; I said, "Yeah, that grand finale was amazing." I said, "No, thank you," to the extra fifty-cent sprinkles. Jelly was there with her family, so we all said hello to them. Her brother, Erik, talked with Mom about how much he was loving quantitative analysis at college while Jelly and I chatted with Ziva Marks, a friend of ours from school. She was having a few people over in two weeks, before she left for a summer program at Johns Hopkins, where she'd be studying journalism. We talked about SAT prep and how many APs we were going to take in the coming year, and the AP Latin teacher's reputation as a space cadet.

There was no reason I should feel claustrophobic, chatting with friends under a clear summer sky with ice-cream cones in our hands. Okay, Ziva Marks is a total, unabashed nerd, with her terribly cut hair and schlumpy clothes, all giggly about weird stuff like memorizing the periodic table and the names of every Webkinz stuffed animal ever made, but really she is a sweet and generous friend, with a hilarious sense of humor if you catch her references. And Jelly Chen is a smart, witty, lovely girl, and my best friend. Jelly Chen is just like me—polite, focused, responsible.

Ah. No wonder I was light-headed and sweating. I wasn't a big fan of myself at that moment, either. Anyway, I was tired and sticky and just really ready to go home. But my family was lagging as my two closest friends discussed whether it would be more fun at Ziva's party to play Pictionary or watch a *West Wing* marathon. Maybe instead we should just watch *1776* again?

"Whatever," I said. "Any of those."

"They're all fun!" Ziva squealed. "Maybe we'll do a little of each? And eat those little pretzels shaped like portcullises?"

"I love those!" Jelly shouted. "Wowzers!"

"I gotta go," I said. It was not just seeing Allison and Tyler talking up the hill, or him chasing after her when she stepped away from him. What was he telling her? *God, no.*

Phoebe and Dad were talking to Phoebe's boyfriend, Luke, and his dad in front of the hardware store. Dad's laugh ricocheted off the store windows and joined the echoes of the fireworks. Mom and I leaned against Dad's car and waited for the rest of them.

"So Jelly's having a party?" Mom said. "That should be fun."

"No," I said. "Ziva Marks. Not Jelly. Allison!"

I told myself not to think about it, not to wonder why I was so annoyed at Mom for getting it wrong or about why I was dreading this nerd-fest of Ziva's, despite the fact that

I actually fully love *The West Wing* and Pictionary and *1776* and little pretzels shaped like portcullises.

"But you'll go with Jelly? Is that what you said?"

I just said, "I guess. Sure. Are we ready to go? Allison! Come on! Let's go!"

"It's nice that she's around this summer," Mom said. "You always liked Jelly; you should hang out with her."

"I do hang out with her, Mom!"

"And isn't Ziva the one who won the spelling bee?"

"That was Jelly," I said. "Ziva won the geography bee."

"I thought you won that," Mom argued.

"We tied," I said. Tyler was holding Allison by the arms and whispering to her. I thought my head might spontaneously combust, so I shouted, *"Allison! Come on!"*

"Shut up, Quinn!" Allison yelled back. But she did yank herself away from Tyler and stomp to the car.

"What did he say?" I asked Allison, dreading the answer.

"Nothing," Allison said.

"I don't trust him," I whispered preemptively.

"Because he's a boy?" she asked. "Or because he says he loves me?"

"He said that?" I asked, feeling my fingers go numb.

Allison shrugged, but the smile she was trying to force into a frown was having none of it.

When we finally got home Phoebe chased Allison up

to Allison's room and they closed the door quickly behind them. I could hear Phoebe's voice, all happy and excited, behind the door as I passed it going to my room. *Still my room,* I thought now, each time I entered it. *Still my room.* I didn't even take a shower.

He told her he loves her, I thought.

Well, better than telling her I kissed him.

Ugh.

I was unbearably exhausted and wanted nothing more than to crawl under my covers. I conked out before my head hit the pillow.

I woke up at dawn and watched the sky brighten. Dawn is always my favorite time of day.

When the transition from night was done, I opened my computer and checked my email—nothing, a few status updates from people whose status I didn't really feel like thinking about, an email from Ziva with the subject line PARTY. I didn't open it. Instead I stared out my window for a while. I just felt so vaguely sad; even the clouds tracing their slow route across the sky seemed to mock me, by having somewhere to go.

After an hour of that, I opened my computer again and made a journal file. I decided to write about what was going on, how I felt about it, maybe figure out why I was feeling so prickly lately, plus work on why I had done what I had done (I still couldn't bring myself to name it even in my head), but there was a knock on my door just after I typed the date, so I shut the computer. "What?"

It was Phoebe. In her boxers and rumpled sleep T-shirt, she lingered in my doorway and asked, "Can I ask you something?"

"Yes."

"Why do you hate Tyler Moss so much?"

I sat up and shoved my computer behind me. It was closed and I hadn't even had a chance to write one word about what had happened yet, but I felt totally caught anyway. It took a lot of effort to sound innocent and I was not sure I succeeded. "Who says I hate him?"

"It's pretty obvious, Quinn." She smiled. God, she has the happiest, most winning smile. It was impossible not to smile back a little, even then.

"I think it really matters to Allison that you see he's actually a great guy," Phoebe insisted.

"Okay," I answered. "Thanks."

"For what?"

"It's . . . I don't know. That's . . . You're right. I'll try, okay?"

"Great," Phoebe said. "I'm starving. Should we make some eggs?"

"Eggs? So early? What are you even doing awake?"

She checked my clock. "It's nine thirty. Come on, cheese omelette? With fried onions?"

"I . . . Sorry," I said. "I am, um, meeting a friend . . . going for a walk now."

"Oh?" Phoebe half said, half asked. I flipped my hair over my head to gather it in a ponytail, to avoid looking at her.

"Good thing you came in," I added. "I'm running late."

"I miss Gosia already," Phoebe said, and sniffled. "I can't believe—"

"I know," I told her. "Me too. Just don't say anything to Mom and Dad, okay? They're already—"

"Mad stressed, I know," Phoebe said. "I'm not a baby."

"I didn't say you were," I assured her.

"I was just telling *you*," she added. "Not them."

"Okay." She was leaving my room as I opened my underwear drawer. The heel of one of Mom's shoes poked out.

"How is nobody else hungry in the morning but me?" Phoebe was mumbling.

I shoved a bunch of socks on top of the shoe. "I don't know, Phoebe, okay? I'm sorry, I just . . . I can't answer all your questions right now."

"It wasn't that kind of question. You don't have to answer."

"Rhetorical," I said.

"Talk about mad stressed . . . jeez, Quinn. You don't have to bite me, you know?"

"Sorry." I yanked on a tank top and shorts and left the

house with no plan of where to go. I am not a jogger, so that was out. There was no actual friend for me to meet. I did need some air, though, so I decided to take a walk. Then I wouldn't have totally lied to Phoebe, I tried justifying to myself on my way down the driveway.

That was my plan, and I was kind of happy with it. Despite my usual lack of interest in anything that might cause me to sweat, I was weirdly pleased with this early-morning jaunt. I thought maybe I would do this every morning from now on, take a quick two-mile, three-mile walk to wake me up, to hear some birds chirping and smell the honeysuckle and the lilacs. Honestly. I had myself half convinced that this was what I had been needing, that everything—all the stress and inner turmoil and impulsiveness I'd discovered in myself in the past couple of days—would be resolved with a habit of early-morning walks. All resolved.

Solved again.

Do you have to solve something first, though, before you can re-solve it?

But no, no mind games, I told myself. No thinking. I was just walking, just a girl, the only girl in my family with no boyfriend, no boy who ever thought she was worth asking out or even hooking up with except for Mr. Rebound in Love with My Sister, who therefore does not count at all, especially because I kissed him and he just didn't instantly pull away because of maybe, like, misplaced gentlemanliness or even just shock. Anyway. Not thinking about that. Thinking about walking. Thinking about just being nobody, an isolated random girl out for a walk. Randomly. No destination.

Maybe it was in my subconscious, or my unconscious (still can't quite sort those two guys out), but it was definitely not my plan to walk all the way to Oliver's.

11

I TOTALLY WOULD HAVE walked right by, but Oliver was sitting out front on a bench, playing his guitar, and he called to me.

I was not faking a startled reaction.

He patted the seat beside him.

I hesitated.

He waited.

I crossed my arms.

He strummed a chord and sang softly, "Quinn Avery stood on my sidewalk today, trying to decide—walk . . . or stay. . . ."

I couldn't help smiling a little.

"Stay," he said softly.

I felt myself moving toward his front porch. "Hey," I said, sitting down on the Adirondack chair across from him instead of on the bench next to him. I couldn't trust myself not to grab and kiss him if I was in close proximity.

I was a lot less predictable lately than anybody (including I) had realized.

"How's it all?"

"Okay," I lied. "Well, I told you, you know . . ."

"Yeah," he said, strumming lightly.

"They repossessed our piano."

His fingers froze above the guitar strings. "No way."

"Way," I said. Luckily, no tears threatened. I was all cried out.

"That sucks," he said, shaking his head sympathetically.

I smiled.

"What?" he asked.

"Nothing." I half giggled. "It's just, yeah. Exactly." I stretched my legs out in front of me.

"So, what happened? This was all pretty sudden."

I shrugged, very world-weary and sophisticated, I hoped. "The economy," I said. "Plus, I can't really say, but my mom is a very moral . . . She's the most . . . I don't want to say heroic or . . . But—let's just say she took the fall for a lot of jerks."

"Really?"

Oliver was looking with his X-ray-vision eyes at me—not heavy-lidded and intense like Tyler, but sharply focused, reflecting my image back at me from somewhere deep in them. "Yeah." I sighed.

"You must be really angry."

"About what?"

"At her," he said. "Your mom."

I shook my head. He had it all mixed up. "No. Not at all."

"Not at all?"

"She didn't . . . She's completely blameless, for one."

"And for two?"

I smiled. "I don't really get mad."

"Ever?"

I shrugged. "Not really, no."

"Wow, that's a lot of tight control there."

"No," I said. "It's not—it just seems pointless to get mad. You know? You end up losing control, saying stupid things and doing stuff you shouldn't. . . ."

"That would be a sight to see," he said.

I blinked, turned my own eyes down, studied my sneakers. *Give it up, Quinn. You are too old to have little-girl crushes now.* Abruptly, to change the subject, I said, "I think we may have to move."

"Move? Where?"

"I heard them discussing moving in temporarily with my grandmother." I hadn't mentioned this to either of my sisters yet. I hadn't even admitted to myself that I'd heard it, and hearing myself say it aloud to Oliver I heard it, really heard it, for the first time. I bit my lip. This was not good. I was all jumbled up and starting to sweat. Profusely.

Always an attractive flirtation move.

"No!" Oliver half frowned, half grinned. "The grand-mother who hates Allison?"

"She does not! Allison just hates her. It's projection."

"That'll be a party." Oliver put the guitar down and stretched his legs out, too. "I'm sorry I won't be here to witness that."

"Why?" I asked, trying for casual. Failing. "Where are you going?"

"Back to school."

I think I managed to say, "Oh."

He shrugged. "Yeah. I gave it a shot."

"I didn't realize you had just taken . . ."

"Leave of absence. Junior year not abroad. Yeah. So, I'll be a junior."

"Me too."

He smiled. No teeth.

"I mean, obviously . . ." *Oh can I possibly be this lame?* "I'll be in high school."

"I know," he said. "I know you."

"What do you mean, you gave it a shot?" I was talking in a higher key than usual, but it seemed urgent that I get him talking so I could catch up with my racing pulse and not make even more of an ass of myself. Although we'd spent half an hour every week for a year sitting beside each other on a piano bench, his hands sometimes touching mine, his shoulder tantalizingly close to mine, his scent of shampoo and fresh air wafting around us—plus a few minutes afterward chatting in our kitchen, usually—I had never really asked him why he wasn't at Harvard anymore, what he was doing hanging around our town, taking over some of his mom's piano students, including Phoebe and me, but basically just, as far as I knew, loafing. I had wondered all year what had happened with school, but I didn't want to be rude. I didn't want to pry.

Well, I did want to pry, but I didn't want him to think I was prying. But there on his front porch it seemed, finally, like maybe he'd be okay talking about it. And I was determined to stop barfing up embarrassing little pearls about my family and myself. *I'll be in high school.* Jesus freaking Christ in a Buick, as my grandmother would say.

"I mean," I said, truly unable to shut my mouth, "if you don't mind saying—what happened?"

"I had this really great professor. He hated me."

"Sounds awesome." *Did he fail out? Oliver Andreas? Not even possible.*

"He was. Brilliant, intense, so hard. I wrote this fugue for his class, and it was kind of a crazy time . . . you'll see when you go to college. I was just . . . I wasn't sleeping; I was trying to write for the *Crimson*, and study, and then there was marching band, which is actually way cooler than it sounds, and much more work, plus I was playing guitar a couple nights at this little pub in Harvard Square, and I was dead set on having fun, too, which . . . Anyway, so, the beginning of the fugue was really good, but I kind of let it get away from me—I guess I got a little overambitious."

"Why?" I asked. "Did you try to introduce more than three voices?"

"Yeah," he said, his eyes lighting up. "You know Bach's fugues?"

"Not really," I said. "I mean, I like Bach—don't love him, but he's kind of growing on me. So, from listening and, well, you mentioned something about Bach's fugues earlier this year. . . ."

"I did?" he asked.

"I like counterpoint," I admitted. "Well, I haven't really . . . It sounded interesting, so I checked out a couple of books and, well, I kind of read them. So, how many voices did you try to shove into your fugue, then?" I asked him.

"Seven."

"Seven?"

"Yeah. It was my first try at it. But I thought—"

"Uh-huh," I interrupted, forgetting to watch what I said, or to try to seem cool and mature to him. "And for your next trick, maybe you should build a skyscraper, starting at the top floor and working down from there."

He grabbed a flower off the bush beside him and chucked it at me, laughing. "I know, but I, well, I thought it was pretty good—anarchic, you know?"

"Yeah, I know."

"You do, don't you?"

"Yes. I know you."

"Jeez, Quinn Avery."

"What?"

He shook his head. "Well, Professor Glover didn't get it. Or maybe he did get it; he totally got it. He called me to his office and he threw it at me."

"Threw what at you?"

"The score, the music. Literally. He was so steaming mad his face was all red. And then he . . . Well, anyway."

"Tell me!" I demanded.

Oliver sighed. "It'll sound like bragging, but it really isn't, I swear."

"Okay. If you get out of hand, I promise to cut you down to size."

"Deal." He sighed and said softly, "He said if he had my talent, he wouldn't be pissing it away like I was doing. He said if I wanted to be a good-time Charlie, go ahead, but then I shouldn't do music because it was a travesty for me to do it so half-assed."

"So you decided . . ."

"To do it full-assed. Yeah. Well, first to drop his class."

"Good-time Charlie?"

"I know. So," Oliver continued, looking up at the sky, "I gave myself a year. A lot of geniuses, successful geniuses, have dropped out of Harvard: Bill Gates, Stephen Wadsworth . . ."

"Who?"

"Opera director, Juilliard professor, great guy."

"Never threw a score at you?"

Oliver grinned and shook his head. "Couple of puns, maybe a chair."

"That's good," I said. "Juilliard?"

"Took some classes. Applied. Didn't get in."

"Really? That's crazy."

"Not really," he said. "I'm good, I think, but I'm not, you know . . ."

"Brilliant?"

He shrugged. "It confirmed for me that I wasn't getting what I wanted, anyway. I don't even know if I want to do classical or rock. I should know, right? Well, neither one has panned out so far for me. . . ."

"You're good at both," I said. "Maybe you're just too brilliant for people to understand."

He looked at his feet, bare in tattered old untied running shoes. "I had this idea about myself," he said, and hesitated.

"It doesn't sound like bragging." I got up and went to sit beside him. "It sounds like . . . I mean . . ."

"Like what?"

"Like me, when I'm just thinking. Alone. About myself. Not that I'm at your level of, well, anything, but . . ." *Urgh! Could somebody please come shove a sock in my mouth?*

"I'm not so sure about *that*," he said gallantly, as I cringed.

"Tell me what your idea of yourself was."

He sighed. "I . . . I just . . . I had this idea I was . . . that it was all going to just . . . happen for me. To me."

"I am familiar with that idea," I said slowly.

He nodded. "I bet you are, Quinn Avery."

We sat there for another few minutes, staring straight ahead. Nobody had ever said out loud my own thoughts about myself like he just had. I mean, he was way more talented at piano than I could ever even dream of being, but he just sounded like . . . me. Inside me. Secret me. But the boy version, I guess, deeper voice, college, music. Same theme, two voices: a fugue.

I didn't want to say that out loud, despite knowing on some level he would totally get it and not think I was being a sap. Still, though, I tucked it away, saved it for someday, for maybe.

"Maybe it still will," I whispered, still looking straight ahead, afraid to move much. "Happen for you."

"I hope so," he said. "But hoping is not a strategy. I don't know. I have this friend who says if you never fail, you aren't trying hard enough." He turned toward me, so I turned, too, and we were looking into each other's eyes then. His were dark, and sad around the edges, more closed now, more internal. "Maybe I just finally tried hard enough."

"Your friend sounds like a really smart guy."

Oliver laughed. "Actually he's a wastie in the pub I

play in sometimes. But maybe he's wise. I don't know." He leaned back again and I realized his arm was around the back of the bench, behind me.

"A friend of mine . . ." I started.

"Yes?"

"Not really a friend."

"Okay." He looked a bit amused. I ignored that.

"He was like, 'No big deal,' about the piano. 'It's just things,' he said. Which, obviously, but . . ."

"Right. And we're just blood and hormones."

I felt my shoulders loosen. "Right." I leaned back and could feel the heat from his arm, not touching my shoulders, but near. "And music is just noise."

"Your boyfriend?"

"No!" I didn't mean to shout. "No. Allison's, actually. I think. They broke up, but I think they got back together. Last night. Not that . . . Anyway, I don't like him very much."

Oliver's eyebrows went up. "No?"

"Shut up," I said.

He held up his hands in surrender. I felt my face heating. *Don't take your arm away.*

He let it fall back down again to the back of the bench. His thumb grazed my shoulder, maybe by accident. Or maybe not. "Quinn," he said quietly.

I turned again to him, as innocently as I could. "What?"

He just looked at me for a few seconds, then said, "That sucks about the piano."

I nodded.

"And everything."

I nodded again.

"And . . ."

And then I felt my face moving toward his. He wasn't moving away. *Holy crap, I am going to kiss Oliver,* I thought, and then immediately, still moving microscopically toward him, I had two more simultaneous thoughts: *What the heck has happened to me this week, when I never kissed anybody before and now I am practically attacking unsuspecting boys at every opportunity,* and also, *What if he pulls away like "Ew, little girl, what the heck are you doing?" How awkward would that be? Can a person actually die of embarrassment? Because if so I would keel over right into his mother's hydrangeas.*

I stood up. "Gotta go," I barked out, and, without looking back, trotted stumblingly down his front steps and out to the sidewalk, took a quick right, and zoomed away, not realizing until too late that I had gone the wrong way and would have to loop around the whole block to get home.

It took a while, which was why I wasn't there until too late.

12

Here is the thing about a real estate open house. It is kind of like a doctor's appointment. Instead of your body being checked out, of course, it is your home; instead of a doctor, who presumably went to school for a very long time and studied ridiculously hard and also has professional ethical requirements concerning the patient's privacy and well-being, you get whoever the hell has nothing better to do on a Saturday afternoon than rifle through somebody's stuff, making faces and comments and judgments.

Before a doctor's appointment you (if you are me) take extra care in the shower so your nails are clean and you smell good, even if you have a fever and have to brace yourself on the shower walls because of dizziness. If you have an open house, you basically do the same, but on a housewide level. Whatever is not cleaned up because you were out flirting with a completely unavailable and by all appearances kind but uninterested college guy, so you barely have time to make your bed—whatever is still not neatened to your crazed family's standards by the time the clock strikes noon has to be shoved somewhere it is hoped (but should not be believed) the rampaging vultures will not open.

They will open it anyway.

When the economy is bad, nobody is supposed to have enough money to buy an overly big, overly luxurious house like this. The extras, the marble and the granite and the Bosch, Sub-Zero, warming drawers and media room and mahogany and wet bar, are all *très* passé, but apparently word of that did not get out, or perhaps word of that was overwhelmed by words like *fire sale* and *must sell NOW* or just plain damned curiosity.

For a while in the spring Allison had this thing where she was convinced she'd sold her cell phone to the devil. Or maybe she was kidding; it is extremely hard to tell with her and her drier-than-Mom's-martinis sense of humor. But if the devil had come along during the open house and made me an offer to sell my cell phone, or my soul, to clear the people out instantly, I would have done it. I swear I would have. For so many reasons.

And the "it's just stuff" argument would not persuade me, either. Somebody went through my medicine cabinet. My tampon box was taken out and left on my counter.

Ew.

They opened everything.

"There are no ethics in an open house," Mom murmured to Dad. "No levels of discretion."

He said, "Let's go for a walk."

After they came back and the last of the vultures were shooed away, the exhausted-looking real estate agent collected her clipboard and her offering sheets and shook my parents' hands. She smiled and said, "I think it went great!" and retreated in her beige-on-beige Jaguar. "We'll talk."

Dad offered to get a pizza.

Nobody was hungry.

I went up to the guest room, not just to check my email or listen in on the baby monitor to spy on my parents. I was tired; I wanted to be alone. Okay, also to spy. And maybe to check my email.

The only one I got was from Tyler Moss, asking, *You okay?*

Fine, I answered immediately, my heart weirdly pounding. I almost added, *How about you?* to be polite, but I so didn't want to get into it. I deleted the thread immediately after I hit SEND, and phew on that, because as it was deleting itself, Allison and Phoebe barged in. I slammed my computer closed and looked at them as innocently as possible.

"Did they say anything yet?" Phoebe asked.

"Not . . . I wasn't really . . ." I turned up the volume on the monitor, but it was only static. We watched it for a minute, which was weird because it's not like there was video; it was just a white-and-blue plastic baby monitor. We waited for it to morph into something else, I guess, but it didn't.

"Are you going to the party tonight?" Allison asked me.

"Yes," I said. "No."

"Are you sure?" Phoebe asked, with a smile in her voice.

"Positive," I answered. When did she get to be so witty, little Phoebe? "What party?"

"Max Kaufman's," Allison said. "Obviously."

"Obviously," I echoed. "No. I'm just going over to a friend's house."

"Jelly's?" Phoebe asked. "Oh, I love her. Can I come with you? I could cancel my thing. Are you going to the movies? Because I am so in the movie mood. But if you guys are just going to be, like, doing math or something, forget it, I guess. Is that what you guys are doing?"

Before I could respond to that, Allison said, "Tyler will be disappointed you won't be there," and I swear my heart seized up.

"Why?" I asked her, or maybe demanded. "Why—why do you say that?"

"I swear he has a crush on you."

"Shut up!" *Oh, God, oh, God, oh, God.*

"He asked me twice today if you were coming to

Max's party," Allison said.

"No way," Phoebe said. "Twice?"

"Twice."

"Well, they're in the same grade," Phoebe said.

"He doesn't even . . . We barely know each other," I said, willing myself to sound at least a bit less colossally strange.

I consciously relaxed my face, unclenched my jaw, took a deep breath through my nose. My sisters, meanwhile, watched me as if they were seeing a particularly awful reality show. I willed myself not to check my closed computer just to make sure it really was closed and no new emails were popping up from hot boys in my grade who should not be trusted and who might be thinking about me when he so shouldn't be.

"He keeps asking me about you, what we talk about, what you said." Allison shrugged. "I think he's intrigued by you."

Which gave me a coughing fit. Phoebe pounded me on the back while I tried to convince my spasmodic larynx not to kill me in front of my sisters.

"Seriously," Allison was going on, without regard to my hypoxia. "Roxie the other day said anybody as strait-laced as you is probably sick kinky."

"Ew!" Phoebe and I said at the same time.

Allison laughed and went to adjust the baby monitor on the night table. "That's what I said, but Roxie was like, 'Yeah, trust me on this,' and Tyler, I think, agreed, because since then he keeps asking me stuff about you—if I saw you, if we hung out. Seriously."

"Your friend Roxie is a sick pup," I managed, signaling Phoebe to stop pounding my back by jumping up onto the bed, away from her surprisingly strong hands. "And Tyler," I said, narrowly avoiding toppling myself off the bed by grabbing a pillow at the sound of his name, God help me. "I mean, he's cute but, Allison, I don't think you can really trust—"

"Okay," Allison said. "I'm not asking your advice on him. But still I'm glad you'll be otherwise involved, and not just lusting distantly over Oliver Andreas anymore."

"Oliver is so cute, though," Phoebe said. "In a slightly nerdy way, but don't you think he'd be the perfect guy for Quinn?"

"Ew," Allison said. "He babysat us. And he's in college, hello?"

"He's not that old," Phoebe argued.

"Nineteen," I said. "And I'm almost seventeen."

"Whatever," Allison said. "Go for it then, if you think he's so perfect."

"Sure," I said. "Like that's even a possibility."

"Why not?" Phoebe asked.

"Why do you even like him so much?" Allison asked.

"Um," I said. "Because he's . . . brilliant?"

"So are you," Phoebe said. "So, there you go!"

Allison rolled her eyes. "Eye of the beholder, I guess. Good to know we can totally not overlap on guys. To me Oliver Andreas seems a little impressed with himself, like he needs to be brought down a rung or two, honestly."

"That is completely untrue," I started to argue, but then, luckily (I thought), Mom's voice came through the static, so we all crowded close, straining to hear.

". . . feels like retreat . . ." she was saying.

My sisters looked at me quizzically.

". . . don't see . . . alternatives . . . Montana . . ." Dad responded.

Phoebe's face paled. "We wouldn't move to Montana, would we?"

"No," Allison said.

"I think we're going to move to Grandma's," I whispered.

They both swallowed hard.

"At least it's here," I said. "We'll be able to stay in school."

Allison got up. "Dandy," she said. "And we'll just bunk in with Grandma and Grandpa? What, the three of us will share Uncle David's room?"

I shrugged. "I guess. Nothing we can do, so we'd better just deal. They have to sell this house. We may as well get used to it."

Tears were running down Phoebe's cheeks. "I don't want to move," she whispered. "It's not fair."

"It has nothing to do with fair," I said. "Is it fair the kids at my camp eat ketchup for dinner? Life's not fair."

"Wisdom from Disney," Allison sneered. "Excellent."

"That's terrible, too," Phoebe whispered. "I don't mean to sound spoiled, but I mean, this is our home."

"No," I said. "It's just a house."

"Well," Allison hissed, "aren't you just the best-adjusted person ever? Screw you, Quinn."

She slammed the door on her way out. I turned to Phoebe, but she wouldn't look at me, either; she got up to follow Allison out.

"I'm just saying . . ." I started.

"I know," Phoebe said, and shrugged, and left, her fingers lingering on the door like she didn't want to let go even of that.

13

THE FIRST SHOCK WAS JELLY. I got into the car and did a triple take. It wasn't just her new glasses, with their thick rectangular frames, or the washed-out blue of her T-shirt dress. She looked different. She looked kind of cool. In a nerdy, funky way—really cool.

She had Adriana's address plugged into her GPS already, so we let Annoying Lady direct us there. When we turned in past the gates at the bottom of her driveway, we were both wide-eyed. The tires crunched delicately over the stones on her long driveway as we made our way toward the huge house looming in front of us, with the sun painting the sky perfectly in stripes of pink and orange behind it.

Adriana's housekeeper escorted us through the house that looked like a hotel in Miami, all modern art and white draped fabric and cool-shaped stuff that might have been tables or stools or possibly sculptures, to the backyard, where Adriana was hanging with a small crowd of people who were themselves draped languorously over big, square, bed-looking things arranged beside her beautiful stone pool, which was lit by floating multicolored lily pads.

"Wow," Jelly said.

"Yeah," I agreed.

"Quinn!" Adriana yelled, unfolding herself from a group of people on the blue cushion thing. "Jelly!"

She came over and gave us each a hug like we were her long-lost aunties. We awkwardly hugged her back.

"Hey, Mason!" she hollered. "Come take some drink orders."

"I thought we're not drinking tonight," answered a six-foot-tall, gelled-hair Adonis, smiling a professionally handsome smile as he approached us.

"You know the rules," Adriana said flirtatiously to him.

"Rules are there for the fun of breaking them," he answered.

"Quinn, Jelly, this is Mason, who is definitely not drinking tonight."

"Hi, Mason," Jelly said, grinning her thousand-watt, inimitable Jelly grin at him.

"Hi," he said to Jelly, as he slipped his arm around Adriana's narrow waist. She whispered something to him and then he turned to me, looking amused, but didn't say anything, and then I couldn't, either. And then, even worse, I jumped and might have made a small squeaking noise, because another guy, right behind me, said in a deep baritone, "You must be Adriana's new friends."

This one had blond wavy hair down to his shoulders and bright, smiling pale eyes.

"Oh, my goodness, it's a swarm," Jelly said, and I had to laugh. Adriana made more introductions (the blond was JD, and he couldn't take his eyes off Jelly) and slipped away casually herself to get us sodas at the bar on the other side of the pool.

"How have I not met you before?" Mason whispered to me, his mouth close to my ear, strangely and suddenly in my space.

"Um," I brilliantly answered. "Well, where do you go to school?"

"Nowhere," he whispered, and I could smell cinnamon on his breath as it touched my hair.

I backed up two steps. "Nowhere?"

"It's July."

"Before this. After this," I said. "I mean, maybe we go to different—"

"I just graduated," he said. "And you haven't even given me a graduation present yet, Quinn."

Adriana showed up with sodas just then. I plopped down next to Jelly, who was cracking up over some story JD was telling her, on the nearest seating thing. There was a couple making out on the other side of Mason. I focused on the can in my hand.

"You seem tense," Mason whispered near my head. "Am I making you feel uncomfortable?"

"No," I said. "Yes. A little."

"Mmmm," he said. "That's good."

As I popped open my can, I inched away from him. He was too close, too good-looking, too insistent. I tried to tell myself this was just what I needed, the perfect antidote to unavailable, off-limits, not-my-type Tyler and unavailable, off-limits, love-of-my-pathetic-life Oliver. Mason. The perfect summer fling, and he seemed more than willing. He seemed interested in me for sure—in fact, he hadn't taken his bluest-blue eyes off me. If I leaned forward two inches we'd be kissing already. I should totally go for it, I told myself, as Jelly's laughter trilled beside me and the can sweated in my hand.

I realized I was slanting away from him, in search of my own bit of oxygen. "Um," I said quietly. "I'm sorry, I'm not . . ."

But before I could explain that I was not actually interested in having this admittedly beautiful guy in my airspace, I was distracted by a clattering across the pool and gratefully turned to see what it was.

It was Oliver.

Laughing.

Walking, with his arm draped gently around a curvier version of Adriana, right toward me.

"What are you not?" Mason was asking beside me, but I couldn't stop myself from staring at Oliver. He looked so happy, so relaxed and at ease with this girl who was clearly Adriana's older sister. I felt my insides caving in, crushing my pitifully enduring hopes that I'd pushed down, away, for so many years, those well-tended fantasies that maybe someday I'd look at Oliver and he'd be looking just like that, but at me.

How long had I been foolishly, subconsciously making excuses to myself? *Maybe he's shy, maybe he's just really focused on his music, maybe he's just different from other guys—*to comfort myself into the continuing illusion that maybe, maybe it's not that he's just not into me, doesn't just think of me as the sweet girl he's known forever who's always had a little bit of a crush on him that she will hopefully soon outgrow. Maybe he secretly likes me but doesn't know quite how to show it yet.

But there he was, circumnavigating the pool, proving he absolutely knew how to show it—when he felt it. His soft laughter was like being stabbed by icicles.

"What's wrong, Quinn?" the boy beside me, Mason, was asking.

"Nothing," I grunted.

Jelly looked away from JD at me, and then followed my eyes to Oliver. Just as she groaned, "Uh-oh," Oliver finally noticed me.

I willed myself to look away from him and smile up at

Mason, whom I totally had no interest in right then but realized a sudden need for. His eyes truly were a magnificent color. I couldn't help noticing Oliver's arm dropping away from Adriana's sister's waist.

That helped generate my smile. "Nothing's wrong," I whispered up at Mason. "What could be wrong in this best of all possible worlds?"

He tilted his head, looking down into my eyes. "You have an interesting way of talking," Mason said. "Slow and a little . . . off."

I was concentrating on maintaining eye contact with Mason despite the sight of Oliver approaching in my peripheral vision. "Off?" I asked softly, not moving.

"Quinn!" Oliver said, looming above me.

I slowly lifted my eyes to him.

He smiled his gradual crooked smile at me, the worst possible thing, because I am so damn allergic to that smile of his.

"Can I talk to you for a sec?" Oliver asked me, and then thrust his hand out. "Hey, Mason."

"Oliver," Mason said, gripping Oliver's hand with his own meatier hand. "How goes it?"

"Fine, thanks. I just need to ask Quinn a quick . . . Quinn?" He held out his hand to me, and without thinking, I took it, like I was going to shake hands with him. He pulled me up instead.

Adriana's sister called to him from the bar, asking what

he wanted to drink. He said he'd be right there. I felt my face heating up again. When would I ever get to the point of not imagining him declaring his true and undying love for me every time he said my name?

Now, I told myself. *That point is now, this second. I am officially over you, Oliver Andreas. Done.*

It actually almost worked. I was able to look at him more objectively, like the houselights had just come on in the theater and there before me stood not some larger-than-life matinee idol but just a guy—just a guy with a spray of freckles over his slightly too-large nose, dark brown eyes, black hair in soft waves curling around his pinned-back ears, not so much taller than I am, looking with fierce intelligence into my eyes.

Oh, crap. Oliver.

I gave him a polite face like I'd give a subordinate of my mother's. "What's up?"

"Quinn," he breathed, but that was not about to change my adamantly steely heart, especially not with Adriana's sister calling his name from across the pool again, and him smiling broadly back at her, promising he'd be right there, before deigning to look at me, his little buddy from back in the day. "What are you doing with Mason Foley?"

"I don't know," I said. "Probably the same thing you're doing with Adriana's sister."

He clenched his jaw. "I doubt that."

"Well, good to see you. Have fun," I said, and started

to turn away. Adriana's sister was on her way toward us with drinks in hand, and I really didn't need to be there for their reunion. There was a very hot guy waiting for me. *Yes, me, Oliver, little Quinn Avery, who has—surprise!— grown up.*

He caught my shoulder with his hand and pulled me toward him. "Don't," he whispered. "I know Mason Foley, okay? I just . . . don't be yet another of his harem, Quinn. You're better than that, okay? I don't want you to get—"

"Hurt?" I finished for him, and the surprise on his face actually made me laugh a little. "Thanks, Dad. Glad you're looking out for me, but guess what, Dad?"

He looked pale and defeated. Good.

"I can take care of myself. So . . ."

"Quinn," he was saying as I walked away.

Forcing myself not to look back, I headed straight for Mason, and within a minute was kissing my second boy ever, and saying the name Mason over and over in my mind as I kissed him, kissed Mason, thinking *Mason* to crowd out the other name that was trying to push its way into my thoughts instead.

14

I WOKE UP WITH SORE LIPS the next morning. I'd been dreaming not about having made out with Mason Foley but about being little again, little and pretty and beloved, with black shoes that clicked when I ran across wood floors in them while wearing a party dress. In the dream, my mother was telling me we were going to Grandma and Grandpa's house, but as in real life, in history, back then she didn't say, *We're visiting my parents.* She called it going home.

I hated that.

I had hated it hugely, ragefully, irrationally when I was little, though of course I never said anything aloud. I'd just leave the room when she said it. *We'll only be home for a few days,* I remember she said to her friend on the phone as I read on the floor beside her in our apartment in London that year we lived there, and I remember thinking, *But we are already home, aren't we?* Allison played with blocks and Phoebe sucked her thumb in her bouncy seat and Mom talked on the phone and I pretended to read, only four but precocious, and already aware of it, proud of the reactions people subtly (they thought) bestowed upon my parents—*She's reading? That tiny little girl?* But when my mother talked on the phone the letters hovered, slurred. I was an eavesdropper before I was a reader.

Home.

She meant it as a general description, of course. We were foreigners living in England for that one year; it wasn't home. Home was the USA, where the people talked the way my parents did.

But she didn't only mean it that way.

Home was *her* home, the home where she grew up with her parents and her older brother. The places where we lived, first in an apartment in New York City and then for those months in London, nine months really, not the year or years I sometimes let people think it was, my childhood in London that I barely remembered beyond my stories of it and those snapshot moments like reading/eavesdropping at my mother's feet—where we lived even when we moved back to the States, back to New York but not the city, to the town where Mom grew up, just beyond walking distance to her parents' house—none of those places were home to her.

That's what made me mad.

Her home wasn't our home, where she was right then with us, with her husband and children. Her home was a memory. It didn't belong to me.

Hearing her say *home* and mean not our home but her old home made me feel profoundly not sturdy.

I never admitted this to anybody.

But waking up that Sunday morning I admitted it to myself, after the dream. Her home, but not my home, and I didn't like when she called that home *home*. It was a betrayal, being mad at my mother for that, being mad at my mother at all, after everything she did, does for us, but there it was. I was mad at her. This *is our home, you jerk,* I thought in the room I woke up in, the stark white room that screamed its betrayal at me all night as I slept and wrecked my dreams. *This is* my *home, and you are taking it away from me.*

I got up and hauled myself into the bathroom to stare at my still slightly swollen lips for a minute or two. Jelly had been so happy about hooking up with JD, who actually did seem like a sweet guy, though not nearly smart enough for Jelly. She pointed out that she wasn't planning to be SAT study partners with him, just to have fun this summer, and why not?

She was absolutely right. I was determined to want the same with Mason. I could still feel the imprint from his strong hands on my back and sides.

Enough thinking about that, I told myself, and took a long, hot shower.

I went with my father to pick up bagels and pastries

to bring to the house my mother grew up in, the house it seemed pretty clear we were going to move to. We listened to music in the car and he sang along in his happy off-key way, and then focused on choosing food in the store. He offered to let me drive on the way home, so I got in on what felt like the wrong side of the car and buckled up. He told me to check my mirrors. "You always want to know where you are compared to what's around you," he pointed out.

"Yeah," I said. "That would be good."

I backed out of the spot. We didn't talk; we focused on my driving. At a light, though, he said, "So it looks like we'll be moving in with your grandparents for a while."

"Yeah."

"You okay with that?"

The light turned green. "I guess." I eased out. "Are you?"

"It's going to be hard for all of us," he said. "Especially Mom. But like everything in life, I guess, it's just temporary. So we all have to . . ."

"I know," I assured him.

"I'm so proud of you, Quinn," he said. "You amaze me, how maturely and lovingly you are dealing with all this. Mom and I really appreciate you."

I fake-smiled and kept my eyes on the road. I ventured a question at the next stop sign. "Are you mad? At all? At her?"

"At Mom?" he asked.

I shrugged and accelerated. "She's the one who—"

"No, Quinn. I'm not mad. She's the one who what? Supported us all these years? Worked in a high-risk industry and didn't succeed a hundred percent of the time? Why would I be angry at that? Why would you be?"

"I'm not." I retreated. "Sorry I asked."

"You'll learn, Quinn, as you grow up, that everything doesn't always go perfectly. And when—not if, when—it doesn't, that's when your humanity is tested."

"Fine, okay, I was just asking. I didn't say I was mad." I kept my eyes on the road and didn't ask my other questions, like, *What if I want to invite friends over after school, when we're living at Grandma's?* Would I be allowed? And how awkward, inviting them to my grandparents' house! Not that I ever really invited people over, but what if I wanted to? What if things went well with Mason, I was thinking (ha, ha, ha, ha, weird thought even to imagine a future with Mason) and we wanted to hang out or, like, mess around after school? Grandma's living room? With the doilies? Yeah, right. Or the room Uncle David's old trophies still decorated, that I'd be sharing with both my sisters? Oh, now that's romantic.

And what about family time, just our little family? We were just not going to have that anymore?

But I didn't say those things. I was mature and loving; I was Zen; I was just what they wanted and expected me to be. My humanity was being tested, and I did not enjoy the implication that I was doing poorly even for a moment on that fricking test.

I did my best to ignore the dagger I could feel stabbing me through the right eye, after I checked my rearview mirror and saw it wasn't there.

By the time we got home, Allison and Mom were screaming at each other. I rolled my eyes at Allison and mumbled that she should just wear something else. "Who cares? Why does it have to be the shredded miniskirt when it's going to annoy the hell out of Grandma?"

Why did she always have to antagonize people?

She flopped into my room, onto my bed, to complain, and I could have killed her. "Allison!" I yelled. "Get out! Okay? I told you to get out and leave me alone! Why do you have to . . ."

"To what?"

"You know exactly."

"What? Wear clothes I like? Is that such a horrible crime, Quinn? Just because I don't dress like a middle-aged housewife?"

"I don't think wearing khaki shorts and a white T-shirt and flats is necessarily housewifey!"

"Well, then you're an idiot!" she yelled. "You are the most annoying person ever."

"Then get out!" I yelled back. "And leave my Sharpie!"

"It's mine!" She stomped out of my room with my

Sharpie in her hand and slammed my door shut on her way out.

Whatever, I told myself. I had no right to yell at her for stealing a Sharpie after what I did. I would have to spend my whole life making it up to her.

I considered, for the thousandth time, coming clean and admitting to her what had happened. It was just wrong to carry around a lie as I was doing. On the other hand, telling her would only hurt her. She was finally feeling good about herself, after years of definitely not. She had tried to do a modeling thing, which didn't work out. She did get a callback, but since she refuses to talk about what happened when she went for her appointment, it's obvious she was rejected pretty terribly. That kind of thing would have sent her into a pit of despair not long ago, but she has sort of come into herself lately, or anyway, that's what I heard Dad saying to Mom the other night, proudly. So the last thing I needed to do was smash her bud of self-esteem. I have been her protector since she was born. Even if it is me I am protecting her from, I would never want to hurt her.

First choice would be to erase what happened with Tyler, of course.

Since that wasn't an option, I'd just have to not unburden myself at her expense. I was in control of that, at least, and it was the least I could do for her.

I just wished she'd make it easier to be nice to her. And

stop saying the word *Tyler* to me. It's going to be such fun sharing a room with her, I thought, and with Phoebe, too, who, okay, is sweet, but right then I hated her anyway.

I hated everybody right then. Including me.

I flopped down on my bed and checked my phone.

Nothing, no messages at all, including nothing from Oliver. Still. Which, fine.

I opened my computer.

No emails from him or from Mason, either, which was also fine. Didn't expect any, since I hadn't even given them my email address.

None from Tyler, either. Thank goodness. The internet is such a time sink anyway. I shut my computer and vowed again not to think about that. I changed into some jean shorts, a black T-shirt, and my old high-top Chuck Taylors. And some lip gloss and black eyeliner. *Who's a housewife? Not me. I spent all last night making out with Mason Foley, thank you very much.*

In the car on the way across town, Allison insisted on having her earbuds in and the volume up, which was so annoying. And Phoebe texted her billion friends, giggling softly when they made whatever witty comments. Texting is so ridiculous. I watched the trees fly backward into the past and dreaded the day, dreaded the future of sharing a room with these two girls I would never befriend if they were in my grade, dreaded the polite smiles I would be forced to force for the next few hours.

And I eavesdropped on my parents as they discussed how right they were to reject the one offensively low offer that was made on our house.

"There will be other offers," Dad said quietly. "We'll do the rest of the work she recommended, we'll hire the whatever, we'll have another open house. It'll work out. And if we have to move out to sell it properly, okay."

"I swear I'd rather burn that house to the ground than sell it for that chump change." Mom shook her head. "Lisa Lenox. That entitled little—"

"Claire," Dad said, and glanced in the rearview at us. I pretended to be lost in thought, staring out the window. *What a fun day this is going to be,* I thought.

It was even worse than I anticipated.

Grandpa was all bellowy annoying humor, slapping willowy Dad on the back, calling each of us his special nicknames and holding our faces as he kissed us to ensure we couldn't escape. Grandma, on the other hand, smiled her tight smile and checked us each out, including Allison's slashed little miniskirt. Mom said, "Don't even start with her; do me a favor, Mom."

Grandma said, "Did I say one word?"

And then we went inside to have lunch.

Grandpa started off by offering Dad a Scotch, which he said no, thanks to, but that didn't bother Grandpa a bit. Dad took his glass of Scotch and followed Grandpa reluctantly into the living room.

Mom stayed behind to help Grandma unload what we'd brought and add it to what she had prepared. There was a plate out on the counter, "For the girls to snack on," Grandma said. There were two slices of cheese and three crackers on the plate, and about six or seven potato chips. There was also a strawberry, sliced in half. My sisters and I stared at the plate, doing the math in our heads.

"If you finish that, there's more," Grandma said, generously.

Allison took all the chips.

"What?" she said when I glared at her. "We need more chips, Grandma."

"All out already?" Grandma asked.

"Imagine that," Allison mumbled, and stuck her earbuds back in as she slumped down at the kitchen table to munch her chips.

Phoebe took one slice of cheese and balanced it on a cracker. I did the same. Grandma, bag of chips in hand, remarked, "Hungry girls." And placed five more potato chips on the plate.

I caught Mom rolling her eyes as she peeled a carrot at the sink, the shreds of carrot skin falling gracefully, like spent confetti onto a paper towel.

Grandma said we could help ourselves to juice if we liked. I poured myself and Phoebe each half a glass of orange juice from the cracked ceramic pitcher she'd put out. The juice was warm. I was just going to cope, but

Phoebe asked sweetly, cloyingly, "Okay if we take ice, Grandma?"

Grandma nodded. "Of course."

I was next to the freezer, so I got us each a cube. They were a little brownish. I tried not to notice. Grandma and Grandpa are not poor; they are very comfortable, in fact. They owned their own contracting business. They just didn't like to be showy. They'd both grown up working-class and talked often about "showy" people, people who bought multiple pairs of shoes at a time, people who thought the opposite of *new* was *bad*.

People like—it was hard to avoid the obvious—us.

As much as I might agree about the grossness of our materialistic culture, dingy ice cubes? Seriously?

Over lunch Grandpa jovially regaled us with many stories of businesspeople he knew who had screwed up even worse than Mom had. Mort Cohen had apparently embezzled funds from his hit-man brother-in-law and hadn't been seen in months. This one fellow who used to own the shop over in Pelham with the die-cut somethings had invested all his money in Betamax technology back in the 1980s, so he and his wife and four fat kids ended up living in a trailer someplace in Florida, and not the nice area of Florida—and this other fellow had shoveled all his money into a retirement fund that turned out to be a big nothing, and that guy, in his shame, tried to kill himself by jumping out the window of his office and only managed to break his nose. Not even a concussion.

"So you think you did bad, honey?" he said to Mom. "You're small potatoes."

"Thanks, Dad," Mom said, cutting her quiche into molecule-sized pieces.

Meanwhile I was trying not to gag from the disgusting juice it was getting harder and harder to swallow.

"Enough," Grandma said to Grandpa.

Grandpa refilled his and my father's Scotches and we cleared the table.

I didn't hear what Grandma muttered about Allison and her hair or her clothes or her attitude or her cell phone that did doorbell chimes and then "Yankee Doodle" in an endless loop throughout the lovely lunch, but I gathered that it was not complimentary. Allison managed to hear her, though, despite the blasting music that was bleeding out of her ears loudly enough for the rest of us to sing along to. She yanked the earbuds out and said, "You know what, Grandma? I know you think I am impossible and ugly, but honestly? You have no idea, and you're old and nasty, and I don't care."

And then she stormed to the front door, flung it open, and galumphed down the steps and across the flower bed, the yard, the other row of flowers, and out to the side-walk.

"That's how you allow her to talk?" Grandma asked Mom.

"Mom, please," Mom said. "Could you not—"

"Do you want me to go after her?" I asked, my jaw gripped tight. I wanted to smash Allison in the teeth, but to be honest I could also happily have taken a swing at my grandmother, to knock her muttering smugness right across the foyer.

"No," Mom said. "Thanks, Quinn. You're so good."

"I'll clear the glasses," Phoebe said quietly, disappearing quickly, the weasel. One small machine gun in my hand at that moment and the whole family'd be full of holes. Especially when the men emerged, looking slightly off balance and clueless.

"Did Back Alley go out for a walk?" Grandpa asked. "Should we all go?"

"Dad," Mom seethed, checking her buzzing Black-Berry. "Could you please stop trying to be helpful? It is backfiring."

"You're setting quite an example there, Claire," he said. "You're like one of the kids, your face always lit by a screen."

"Dad, I . . ." she said without lifting her eyes from whatever urgent message she was reading.

What? I was thinking. *The cops are on their way to handcuff you? Maybe they could bring some reporters and photographers. Because my life is not deep enough in the toilet after all you've done, Mom.* The thoughts startled me. Was I mad at Mom? *No,* I corrected myself silently. *It's Allison's fault.*

And maybe Grandma's. Not Mom's.

"Maybe we should talk about where the girls are going to sleep," Dad said, his words slightly slurred. Dad was not a drinker, and his half a glass of Scotch had clearly gone right to his head.

"Jed," Mom said, and passed him her BlackBerry.

"What?" he asked, not noticing. "I was just, woo . . ."

Mom took his Scotch and downed the rest of his drink in a gulp. I stared at her. I didn't know if I was more surprised by her ease with the Scotch or the continuing vehemence of my anger at her. *You gonna get drunk now, Mom?* I heard myself think. *On top of everything you are now going to start drinking, too?*

"Did somebody take my soup cubes?" Grandma called from the kitchen.

"Mom, for goodness' sake, nobody stole your damn soup, okay?" Mom yelled. "How hard do you want to make this on us?"

"She'll meet us at home?" Dad asked Mom. "Is she nuts? It's about nine miles."

Mom shrugged and shook her head. "I can't . . . What do you suggest, Jed? How many things can I . . . At least she texted me, right? I am trying to focus on . . . What?" she demanded of Grandma, who was standing in front of us, her lips pursed, holding out the ice cube tray I had taken four ice cubes out of earlier.

"What?" Mom asked her again. "The kids used ice?

Mom, what? They can't have ice? Fine. No ice, kids. Damn it, Mom. Don't torture me. Don't . . . don't be all passive-aggressive; I can't stand it! We'll find another plan. If you don't want us to move in with you, I don't know why you offered."

"It's not ice," Grandma said. "It's soup. It's frozen chicken soup."

I had just taken my final gulp of orange juice in an attempt to keep from blurting out what a jerk I thought everybody was. As a result, I had a mouthful of orange juice/thawed soup. With my tongue I felt a chunk, which, I realized, was not superthick pulp but rather a stewed onion or maybe a piece of celery or turnip or chicken thigh. The explosion of juice/soup out of my mouth all over Grandma's foyer carpet was a shock to us all, though, in my opinion, completely justified.

Grandpa, for one, thought it was hilarious.

We left a bit earlier than planned, Mom clenching her teeth, me and Phoebe and Dad all a bit green, and Allison on a long, pissy hike across town, during which she texted me and confided that she was actually going to Tyler Moss's house, and if I wanted I could meet her there; she'd really appreciate that.

Sure. As if that were even a possibility. What fun. I turned off my phone.

15

I WOKE UP THE NEXT MORNING absolutely, resolutely cheerful.

Adamantly cheerful.

I was so damned cheerful, any negativity that dared encroach on my space would get punched in the nose. That's how fricking cheerful I felt.

I didn't know if I'd had a dream or what, but my eyes popped wide open at five fifty-five, which I took as a good omen because five is my lucky number, and I knew what I had to do:

I had to be my very best self. It was so obvious I spared three seconds wondering why I hadn't seen it before. But then I moved on. Because I was cheerful!

I just needed to be my best self. Isn't that what everybody always advises? I think it was Gandhi who said we are more afraid of our power than of our powerlessness, or something like that. And Gandhi is my freaking hero! Here I'd been sinking into gritted-teeth annoyance and petty resentments, fearing—no, dreading—my powerlessness: losing my home, losing my image of Mom, losing my grip on myself as a good and moral and gifted person. But I was just looking at everything the wrong way, which was why I had been acting so badly, doing such flesh-crawling stuff as kissing two boys. Obviously!

I smiled and got up, brushed my teeth a double round, and then got into the shower, where I lathered, rinsed, and repeated. Vigorously. All while thinking, *Life will throw at me what it will. But meanwhile I will hold my head up. I will remember who I am, who we are. We are the Avery family. I am Quinn Avery. I have a piano recital to practice for, and tests to ace, and disadvantaged children to influence positively. I have my eyes set on the horizon of the Ivy League, possibly Harvard, but Yale or Brown would also be good choices for me, and all it will take is hard work, nailing the SATs and ACTs and SAT IIs, which is just a matter of working on it, no problem, and then I just have to manage an excellent audition tape to submit along with my applications, which I am already working on.*

Good, water off. And about paying for college? That should not be a problem, really, I realized as I towel-dried my hair. Dad worked his way through college. Mom was proud of never having asked for spending money from her parents. I didn't need them to provide everything for me on a silver platter. I didn't even want them to. And I had an easy way to make some cash—trumpeters and cellists and even, yes, oboists like Jelly always have to pay pianists to practice with them and accompany them to auditions, even for stuff like when they try out, in September, for all-state and all-county band and orchestra. So that would be quick and easy money. And fun, too! I was getting more cheerful by the moment!

So there were no problems ahead, with the possible exception that I was starting to levitate, I was so helium-ified. But I wasn't even worried about that. The day, the sky, my future—all were bright and clear. Things were better than ever, actually.

I even made out with Mason Foley, I thought as I whipped my hair back into a tight ponytail. *He'll be in college next year. Maybe we'll hook up again soon and we'll end up falling in love and I will visit him wherever it is he's going to college, and maybe I'll apply there, too; no need to be a snob—the Ivy League is not the only game in town. There are tons of good schools, and getting a good education is mostly about attitude and your own aptitude anyway. Maybe Mason is actually very artistic and intelligent, not just deadly hot, and all the people who misjudge him will realize he wasn't a male slut or whatever Oliver was warning me against; he was just searching for me all this time, and his untapped inner depths will come out to join his outer stunningness, and we will live happily and brilliantly ever after.*

I was, perhaps, looking a bit too far ahead. I get slightly manic when my head clears after a funk.

Luckily nobody was in the kitchen when I got down-stairs, so I escaped with my buzz intact.

Jelly talked the whole way to camp about JD and how they'd texted all Sunday. She needed some reassurance that bad spelling meant nothing. So I reminded her of the fact that Ziva, one of the smartest people in our grade, was a terrible speller. JD's overuse of emoticons was a little disturbing, but we decided he was just being flirtatious, which is a good thing. He was cute, and it was a summer fling, right? Mason was really awesome, too, we agreed. We were so lucky! There was not a lot more to say, because I didn't want to go into Mason's creeping, insistent fingers on my waist. So I told her my family was planning to move in with my grandparents, who needed some help and com-pany. Jelly is really close with her grandparents, who live with them, so she totally understood that. I discussed my ideas about how to redecorate Grandma's house to make it completely comfortable and cool for all of us, with drop-down desks in the living room and one of those beds that turns into a bookcase in the daytime for Mom and Dad in the dining room so we could spread out more.

"That sounds perfect," Jelly agreed, making the big turn into the camp entrance. "Because nobody has a din-ner party while everybody's sleeping!"

"Exactly," I said. "Plus, that way we can fit the upright piano in there, too, no problem."

"Sounds great, Quinn," she said, quieter. "Are you really okay, though?"

"Of course!"

"And your mom?"

"You know her," I said. "She's amazing. Nothing fazes her. She's already making deals, totally psyched. She's actually relieved, I think. Plus, we're all getting more time together, which is really nice."

I was a little out of breath.

"Well," Jelly said, "that's all good. You're pretty amazingly resilient, too, my friend. But if you need some time to, like, get away for a night . . . ?"

"Thanks!" I said. "But I am really great!"

Ramon surprised me, not by slipping his hand into mine as we walked toward the volleyball court, because he always liked to hold my hand as we walked; what surprised me was when he said, "You okay, Quinn? You seem sad today."

"Me?" I said. "No, Ramon. I am actually happy today. Really happy. How are you?"

"¿Qué sé yo?" he muttered. "You seem sad to me." And he pulled his hand away.

What did he know? Nothing. Just a five-year-old kid with wise, old-soul eyes. I smiled at the other campers and organized a game of tag while we waited our turn at the volleyball net. I would not be brought down by a melancholy five-year-old.

While the kids played tag, Adriana and Jelly and I talked about what a great party it had been. I could tell Adriana felt really good about her fixing-up skills, or maybe she was just happy for us—or at least Jelly, that it was really clicking between her and JD. She told me not to worry about Mason not contacting me afterward, because he was notorious for that—but she assured me he seemed very into me and would definitely want to hook up with me again, maybe at the party we should all go to the next Friday night. Everybody would be there.

A headache was starting over my right eye. I pretended I was just squinting in the sun and answered sure, she could text Mason and confirm that he was going to that party, and mention she was talking me into going. Why not? Yeah, I was for sure interested in hooking up again.

Adriana texted him something. She wouldn't show me what, but showed me his response, which I noticed came back immediately: He texted back a winking face.

Later in the day, when Adriana and Jelly were going on, again, about how JD was so fun, even if all he was really into was rowing crew, and about Adriana's boy-friend, Giovanni, whom she spent not just her own party making out with, but the whole next day with at the beach, my weekend was starting to feel in retrospect a bit lame, and maybe with the muggy heat and the energy all my bright, determined optimism was taking, I was wilting a bit. Jelly whispered to me, "You sure you're okay, Quinn? You seem really . . . I don't know . . . stressed."

"Yeah," said Adriana. "What's up? You can tell us."

"No, nothing," I said. "I just . . . I'm getting a little

headache. The sun is so . . . ."

"Yeah, true," Jelly said. "You want to come over after camp and just maybe hang out or something? My parents will be at work, so they won't be bugging us to do vocab flash cards or anything. . . ."

"I don't know." I separated two kids who were fighting and then plopped down next to Adriana and Jelly again.

"No," Jelly was saying. "I don't think so."

"Don't think what?" I asked.

"You look like a girl with a guilty conscience," Adriana said. "Did you and Mason go further than you're telling?"

"No!" I said.

"Told you," Jelly said. "Just . . . I think Quinn's going through . . . I just mean maybe she might need a little space, so maybe we should . . ."

"I still think she did something she's not telling us," Adriana guessed. "Am I right? What'd you do, Q? You can tell us."

What can I say? I liked the idea that she called me Q, as only Jelly had before, and how she was whispering with me, and didn't think maybe I was stressed about boring, tight, nerdy stuff or huge, humiliating, life-shaking things.

"Something pretty awful," I admitted.

They both leaned forward with wide, excited eyes.

"Tell us," Adriana urged.

"What happened?" Jelly asked.

So I told them about Tyler Moss. I left out the part about the piano getting repossessed and about me crying. I just said that my sister, my younger sister, was going out with the hottest guy in my grade and had dumped him, and he came over to our house the other day, after she'd dumped him, and one thing led to another and I had totally made out with him.

Adriana opened her mouth wider than a hippo's and screamed and pushed me in the shoulders and whispered, "No way," all the stuff I always see those kinds of girls doing. She wanted to know what was I going to do and warned, "You can never tell your sister; that would just be hurtful to stop yourself from feeling guilty but wouldn't help—it would be a disaster!"

"I know it," I said. *My thoughts exactly.*

"Well, but the important question," Adriana said. "Was he a good kisser?"

I opened my own mouth wide at the horrible unseemliness of that question and then had to nod. Yeah, he was. Not that I had all that much to compare him to, but, holy crap, yeah, he was a pretty darn good kisser.

"He looks like he'd be a good kisser," Jelly said, her voice quiet and tight. "But Quinn . . ."

"You know him?" Adriana asked, her voice tinged with jealousy.

"Of course," Jelly said. "He's been in my class since

kindergarten, and he was hot even when the rest of the boys were all about Hot Wheels and Pokémon and worms."

"As hot as Mason?" Adriana asked.

Jelly shrugged. "Jeez, Q," she said. "I don't want to be judgmental or anything, and you know I think you are the most moral person ever, but, I mean, poor Allison!"

"No, it's not like that," I assured her. "It was just a mistake between us. He loves her. I really think he does. We just, you know, accidentally kissed."

Adriana shrieked. "That is just . . . Accidentally kissed! So excellent!"

"How do you accidentally—" Jelly started.

"God, it's epically hot. Accidentally kissed your sister's boyfriend."

"Yeah," I interrupted, facing only Adriana. "So, but anyway, we were at my grandparents' yesterday and Allison bugged out and left, and she went to Ty's house and texted me to please come meet her there, but of course I couldn't—the last thing I want to do is be anywhere near him—so I was all like—"

"Wait," Adriana said. "Ty? Tyler Moss?"

"Yeah," I said, going cold. "You know him?"

"Yes! Tyler Moss? Holy crap. This just gets better!"

"Shhh," I said. "Listen, you can't tell anybody. Okay? Please promise me you'll never—"

"Quinn! Tyler Moss? He is so friggin' hot it's sick!"

"I know," I said. "Hence the problem."

"Did she just say *hence*?" Adriana asked Jelly.

"She says stuff like *hence*," Jelly mumbled. I realized she was refusing to look at me.

"That's awesome," Adriana said. "My IQ is skyrocketing just hanging with you smarties this summer. But I had no idea you were so . . . Ty Moss!"

"Shhh," I begged. Volleyball was ending and we had to head to snack, but en route Adriana was telling me that Tyler Moss's cousin went to her school or something. He'd been at the party she'd gone to July fourth.

"Hold on, hold on," she said as we passed out ice-cream cups. "Does your sister have short, spiky hair and amazing gray eyes?"

"Yes," Jelly said, her face a mask of serious blankness. "Allison. She's great, really intense and really vulnerable."

"Wow," Adriana said, not noticing the condemnation pouring from Jelly's every pore. "That's your sister?"

"Yeah," I said.

"Hence," Adriana said. "As of Fourth of July, anyway, I don't think she and Tyler Moss are still broken up."

"I know," I said, sinking again. "They got back together. Wait, she wasn't at a party Fourth of July. She was with us."

"She was there," Adriana said. "She was definitely there. Late night."

"She must have snuck out," I said. "I can't believe her."

"Pot?" Jelly muttered. "Meet kettle."

Luckily, right then my cell buzzed. I checked it, secretly thankful for the escape valve, while Adriana was saying, "Hence you're screwed." And when I saw it was Oliver, I almost had a coronary right there on the deck.

"Is it Tyler?" Adriana asked, standing on tiptoe, craning over my shoulder to see my phone.

"No," I said. "The plot thickens."

"The what?"

"There's this other guy," I started, and they grabbed me and dragged me to the other side of the picnic area, despite the disapproving stare of Syd, the head counselor.

"He's older; he's in college," I said.

"Oh," Jelly said. "Him."

But Adriana's eyes were wide and expectant. "Who? Wait, the piano teacher?"

"Yeah. Exactly. I've had a crush on him basically my whole life, which I have only recently gotten over, because he's totally out of my league. And I think," I said to Adriana, "I think he may be going out with your sister."

"I doubt that," Adriana said, her huge smile glittering. "She's gay."

"She's *gay*?" I asked.

"Yeah," Adriana said, like, how did everybody not know that?

"But she and Oliver . . ."

"Oh, Oliver Andreas?" Adriana asked.

"Do you know *everybody*?" Jelly asked incredulously.

Adriana shrugged and whipped her long hair back into a hair tie. "They're band-geek buddies. Oliver is your life-long crush piano teacher? Really? Oliver Andreas?"

"Yes," Jelly said. "Is he not epically hot enough?"

"Hmm," Adriana said, considering. "I guess I never thought of him like that. But yeah, he is kind of crush-able, in a brooding-poet kind of way, actually. If you're into that. Yeah. You guys might make a cute couple."

"In my dreams," I said.

"Well?" Adriana grabbed at my phone but I yanked it away from her grasp. "What did he say?"

"He wants to know if I want to come over after camp today to . . ."

"To what?" Adriana shrieked. "What perfume are you wearing, girl?"

"To practice piano," I said, trying to sound very *no big deal* about it.

"Oh, man, that is a total move," Adriana said. "You have to go."

I texted him back that I'd be there.

"You are having the best-ever summer, aren't you?" Adriana asked me.

Ha, ha, ha, ha, ha, ha, ha.

16

Nobody was home when I got there, so I was lulled into thinking it would be a quiet afternoon of resisting the urge to rush straight to Oliver's house or to build up his invitation into something more exciting than it probably was.

I should have left right away and maybe everything would have turned out differently, at least for a little while.

Gosia always used to be around, though, and my sisters, too, and usually Dad, by the time I got home from whatever activities I was doing. It was like the house was losing us already, I thought, but then pushed that aside. No! It was good to have some solitude. I liked solitude, I reminded myself, and though I had sort of lost the momentum of cheerful mania from earlier, I managed to convince myself it was, at least, nice to have the house to myself.

That's why I lingered.

This is nice, I thought.

Which reminded me of how my fifth-grade English teacher had outlawed the word *nice*.

"It means nothing," she told us. "It's a nice shirt? A nice girl? A nice day? What the heck do you mean? Is it low-cut, tight-fitting silk shantung in a peach that picked up the color of her blushing cheeks and threatened to reveal sweat moons under her arms? Now we're talking."

The room full of ten-year-olds regarded her blankly, blinking.

But I loved it. At lunch afterward, I sat among my chattering friends in front of my untouched tuna sandwich on its lily pad of tinfoil, thinking about the blushing girl. I knew that girl was hiding something, whenever I thought or somebody used the word *nice*. Since that day, I have often wondered nonsensically what secrets she was keeping, despite the fact that this not-nice girl existed only as part of a vocab lesson.

Wandering slowly up the front stairs, languorous in my solitude in my big house, I continued thinking about being ten and in Mrs. T's classroom. Mrs. T was the first teacher who'd used the word *gifted* to my face. I will never forget that last day of fifth grade, I was thinking as I wandered past my room toward my parents' room. Mrs. T called me aside at recess. There was something she wanted to say to me.

And she wanted me to listen, and to remember.

I did, and I did.

She said I was brilliant. She said she'd been teaching for forty-two years (six times seven years, I remember thinking, fleetingly), and she'd never had a student quite like me. She knew I was brilliant from the first week, and had expected to discover, all year, what type of brilliant I was. "Usually it's easy," she told me. She'd had brilliant math kids and brilliant writers and brilliant artists, even brilliant entertainers and diplomats pass through her classroom, and she'd gotten really good at identifying their brilliance. But I had stumped her, apparently. She didn't know what I would be brilliant at, and, she predicted, I would have moments ahead of me when I felt like a faker, or like a mediocrity. But she wanted me to remember that she told me, on the last day of fifth grade, that I was brilliant, and that she was confident I would someday figure out how to harness my brilliance.

"That's all," she said. "Now go play."

Sure.

I remember being dazed the rest of the day, even that whole summer, maybe. I went off to camp wondering if I was a brilliant swimmer or tennis player, macramé artist or color warrior. I was a good reader, I knew, a bookworm, really, and I was good at music and most school things. But being a good student is not the same as being *brilliant*. So, was I really? Was she wrong? Or was I just missing something?

So I started playing violin and switched to piano when

it was clear I wasn't Mozart, didn't even know how to hold the bow correctly, and couldn't make a decent sound. At least piano sounded good, if tinkling and small under my rubbery fingers. But Oliver's mom was a good and patient teacher, and I practiced so much she thought I had talent. Maybe I did. Hard to say.

And here I was, almost seventeen, and I still hadn't figured out what I might be brilliant at. At being a good girl, maybe, though, wait, no, not even that. I stood in the middle of my white room and felt the air all around me as I smelled the whiteness and listened to the silence. Even though I was trying to empty my mind, I realized actually I was imagining how Oliver would react if I showed up in my mother's stunning fuchsia stilettos and a short skirt, hair down around my shoulders, dangly earrings even— instead of my normal T-shirt, shorts, sneakers with short socks, ponytail.

I opened my underwear drawer and yanked out my ponytail at the same time. I cleared away all the bras and panties that were hiding them and there they were, glittery and bright, like forbidden candy just within my reach. I touched the cool satin with my hesitant fingertips.

What the heck, I decided. *I'll just try them on, for fun, and then quickly return them before Mom even notices they were gone. It's the perfect opportunity.*

I placed them on my rug and stripped off my shorts and T-shirt. A white miniskirt left over from last summer was hanging in the back of my closet. I grabbed that and then a pink tank top from my dresser drawer, and slid my feet into the cool shoes waiting patiently for me.

To my surprise, they fit. When my sisters and I had tried on Mom's shoes before, they were huge. Our feet slid forward and our toes were crushed in the pointy front while acres of space followed behind our feet as we tried to maintain our precarious balance. Not now. Those shoes felt made for my feet.

I had taken two tentative steps, standing straight and imagining myself really wearing them out somewhere, walking into a party or Oliver's house with Mom's long saunter and my own hair shiny and straight down my back.

That's when Allison slammed my door open and glared at me with fire and tears in her eyes.

"Allison," I think I said, but maybe I just gasped.

"How could you?" she snarled.

My mouth opened to ask what she was talking about, to stall, but there was no point. I just stood there in front of my younger sister in my pink tank, short skirt, and Mom's high heels, feeling worse than every word she was calling me in her furious mind.

"I actually want to know," she whispered, not blinking, not budging from my doorway, blocking it as if I might try to escape, or like she needed the doorjamb's support to stand, after the stabbing I'd done to her. "How could you make out with my boyfriend? Why? Why would you do that?"

I considered pointing out that she had broken up with him, that she herself had insisted the very morning I kissed him that he was no longer her boyfriend, but of course that was beside the point.

"It wasn't . . ." I started, without a plan. "I didn't . . ." I tried again, revising fast in my mind, but not fast enough. "What did he say?"

Her mouth opened wide and her eyes blazed even fiercer. "You want to make sure your stories match up?"

"No," I said quickly, relieved to tell the truth about something, if only because I hadn't thought of that. "Not at all, Allison. Please just calm down and I will—"

"Don't you dare!" She punched my door. "Don't you dare talk to me in your morally superior, condescending, slow Zen way. Don't you dare!"

"I never said I was—" I started.

"Bullshit!" she yelled back. "You say so with every breath you take! Every look you give me and Phoebe, every oh-so-patient sigh and correction and 'Actually that was in *Richard the Third*, not *Henry the Fifth*, Allison.' Are you kidding me? You are so superior there's no you underneath it! Give me a frigging break."

I backed away, right into my bed, where I plopped down. We stared at each other across the abyss of my room.

"He told me everything, Quinn," she whispered at me, stepping closer, into my room, stepping right on my

148

discarded camp shirt and shorts as she approached. "He told me how you were crying the day I had dumped him and he was coming here to talk to me, to assure me about his feelings, to tell me he loves me, Quinn. That's what he came over for. But you, the center of the universe, took his kindness as a come-on, and you kissed my boyfriend. He pulled away from *you*, Quinn; is that right or was he lying? Do you have a different side of the story to tell me? Because I want to hear it. I don't know who to believe. My head is spinning."

Her voice cracked. She clamped her jaw shut and took a sharp breath in through her nose.

She stood right in front of me.

I couldn't talk.

"If Tyler is lying you have to tell me, Quinn."

I swallowed. "He's not lying."

She unclenched her jaw. A tear dropped out of her eye. She wiped it away with the palm of her hand, leaving a dark smudge across her cheekbone.

"Thanks for that," she whispered. "Okay."

I nodded once.

She stared at me for another moment as tears brewed in her eyes but didn't spill over.

I opened my mouth to apologize, but before the feeble words could form, she blinked.

Then she said, as calm as I'd ever heard her, "I hate you, Quinn. I will hate you forever for this. You can keep pretending to everybody else that you are good and perfect and brilliant and superior, but you and I will know the truth now. We will know that you are small and jealous and mean. I don't think you loved Tyler, or even wanted him, particularly. I think it just bugged you that somebody chose me instead of you, for once, and you couldn't stand that. You had to have a piece of it, muck it up and smudge it with your fingerprints so it would all be about you."

"Allison . . ." I stopped myself from objecting that no, *she* was the attention hog; everything always had to be about *her*, not me. I stopped not just because I really didn't feel in any position to criticize her right then, but also because I was busy trying to wrap my head around a torqued view of the world that might actually be true. Was that true? Did I make everything all about me? Was she right? Was she seeing the real me for the first time?

"You know what's funny?" Allison was asking me meanwhile.

I shook my head, because honestly I had no idea what was funny.

"He was scared you would tell me what happened, and that he'd come off bad in the telling. Ha! But he doesn't know you like I do, Quinn. I know why you didn't tell me, and even why you didn't blame him. Because you knew I'd see through it, and because you wanted to keep it for yourself, yet another thing that belonged to you and not me."

I shrugged. Maybe she was right; I really didn't know,

and worried she was both right and only scratching the rotten surface.

"I can't believe I've spent my whole life looking up to you," she continued. "Well, not anymore. Every single time I see you, for the rest of my life, I will think of this, of what you did and that you didn't tell me and why. I'll think of how you made me feel right now."

Then she walked slowly across my room, through the doorway, and slammed my door shut behind her.

17

WHEN I GOT MY STUMBLING self to Oliver's, he wasn't there. His mom, my original piano teacher, let me in, with a quizzical look on her kind face. When I explained that Oliver had said I could practice there, she quickly ushered me into their cozy family room, saying, "Of course, of course," but then asking what had happened to our piano.

"We lost it," I said, my voice sounding like it was coming from somewhere else.

She tilted her head, just the way Oliver tilted his, quizzical but quiet.

"Oliver didn't mention you were coming over," she said.

"Is it a bad time?" I stood up, resigned. Yes, of course it was a bad time. It was so thoroughly a bad time.

"No, no, not at all," she said. "Please go ahead. You were always one of my most diligent students. Oliver has said you've made great progress. But don't worry—I won't be eavesdropping. I'll be out back in the garden. You do your work for yourself, now. Don't worry about an audience."

"Thanks," I mumbled. I waited until she had left the room to start. I really wasn't in the mood to practice piano, of all things, but it would've been horribly embarrassing to be like, "Well, actually, I changed my mind," or, worse, "I didn't really want to practice; I just came over to flirt with Oliver. Because I am a shallow, horrible person. Seriously. People are starting to realize the truth."

One of her most diligent students?

I turned the phrase over in my mind. Not one of her most brilliant, not one of her most gifted. Diligent. Ew. A workhorse. How embarrassing. She knew. Maybe everybody knew, Dad, Mom, Oliver—I practiced enough to be decent, even to fool people like my grandfather into thinking I was something special. But I wasn't. I was just hardworking. Diligent.

Maybe I had only been fooling myself that anybody was fooled, and all this time they'd been humoring me. Like when I was little and painted a picture for Mom and she was like, "Oh, Quinn, what a beautiful boat," but it wasn't a boat; it was a man walking his pet cat. "Oh," she exclaimed. "Of course it is! Silly me. What a fantastic picture of a man walking his cat!" But she was holding it upside down. I didn't explain that part; I smiled and let her tell me what an artist I was; because I so wanted it, I was willing to sacrifice the truth for it.

My fingers could barely find the notes of my warm-up scales.

Fake, I was calling myself. *Petty, small, envious, mean. Diligent.*

And where the hell was Oliver?

Wherever he wanted to be, really; he hadn't asked me out on a date or anything; he'd offered his diligent grind of a student a practice space. That was all. It was hard to even remember why I'd fantasized it was anything more.

I considered again just leaving, but it felt rude. I'd have to say good-bye and thank you to Oliver's mother first, and she'd be all like, "That's it? You're practicing for under five minutes?" So I sat my sorry ass on the bench and dutifully played through my scales and then my pieces.

Half an hour later I just couldn't do any more. Diligent? Maybe not even that. I wandered through the kitchen with its blue and white tiles, full fruit bowl, and plate of fresh minimuffins, to the back door. Oliver's mom was kneeling in the midst of a flower bed, cursing in Greek. Not that I know any Greek, but trust me, it was clear.

"Um," I said.

She turned around, startled. "Oh, Quinn," she said. She had a dirt smudge up her right cheek. She explained she had whatever is the opposite of a green thumb and might have overwatered her dahlias to the point of drowning them. She asked if I knew anything about flowers or gardening. I said no and that I had to leave.

She said she'd tell Oliver I'd been by.

I tried to think of a nice way to ask her not to, but she'd already turned back to the patch of mud she'd made. I was halfway through the door when she called to me, asking me to send her best to my mother.

What did she know? Did everybody know what had happened? Did everybody know more than I did about my own family and our Situation? Was there stuff about Mom in the *Wall Street Journal*, even?

I managed a polite smile and said I sure would, thanks so much.

On my way out I impulsively grabbed a minimuffin.

I didn't even want a minimuffin. I don't know what possessed me. I had never stolen anything in my life before that dumb minimuffin. Well, other than Mom's shoes, but they didn't count, because I was completely planning to return them. But the minimuffin? I just . . . I don't know. I wanted to take something, to grab it and wreck the perfect symmetry of the minimuffin pyramid, to steal something that would otherwise belong to Oliver. Or maybe just to steal. Just for perversity. I don't know. I just took it.

Which was why I had a stolen minimuffin in my hand as I was walking out of Oliver's front door and he was walking in.

We both stopped short. We both looked confused, I think. Though only one of us had a stolen blueberry minimuffin in hand. (As far as I know.)

He remembered, suddenly, that he'd invited me to come over to practice. "Oh! Quinn. Sorry," he said. "I . . . This . . . I got—"

"It's okay," I said.

"Did you already practice?"

"Yeah."

"Oh."

"I should . . ." I attempted to angle past him, but as I did, I smooshed the muffin in my hand.

"Wait," he said.

For a horrible moment I thought he was going to demand to see my hands, and when the disintegrating evidence of crushed muffin could no longer be concealed, he'd say, *Caught you red-handed*, the way I used to have a nightmare my father would say, my tender, soft-spoken father-turned-Javert, if I ever got caught sneak-reading under the covers with my flashlight: *Caught you red-handed!*

"You want to go to a concert Saturday?" Oliver asked instead.

"What?" I was off balance and dribbling crumbs onto his porch.

"Beethoven's Quartet in F major, Opus 135," he answered, with such a sweet, excited smile I didn't have the heart to say no; I wasn't asking what they were playing; I was just stalling.

156

"You know the joke in that, right?"

"There's a joke in it?" I asked.

"True," he agreed. "It becomes very much not a joke. You're right."

I actually was not making an erudite point. I was just like, *A joke? Huh?* I thought I ought to clarify, come clean, be honest for once in the month. But I didn't. I said, "Yeah, sounds familiar."

He grinned at me. "It's at five o'clock, so we could . . . I'll pick you up. About like two? So we can get a good spot. I like to be up pretty close."

"Me too." *Wait, is he actually asking me out?* I tried with all my facial muscles to not smile. "That sounds . . . that sounds perfect."

He smiled at me. The earth stopped in its orbit for a second, then another.

"So," he said.

"So," I repeated. "Yeah. See you then."

"Quinn?"

I turned back to him, ready for anything—a kiss, a question, a declaration of love.

"Stuff is falling from your fist."

We both looked at my hand, and at the crumbs raining from between my fingers.

"Sometimes that happens," I said.

He smiled. "Oh," he said. "That's true, I guess. Sometimes that happens."

"Yeah." I could feel my face heating up, so I turned away and jumped down his steps. As the screen door slammed shut behind him, I could hear his laugh echoing inside. It didn't sound like a mocking laugh, though, so even as I rubbed the minimuffin crumbs off my palm onto the sidewalk out front, I wasn't, for once, cringing and criticizing myself.

"Sometimes that happens?" I whispered to myself as I walked toward home. But I was smiling. I was going out on a date with Oliver Andreas. No thoughts of Allison or Tyler or any of my many other complications clouded that thought the whole way home. It was really actually *nice*.

18

"SATURDAY?" MOM ASKED AGAIN.

I shrugged one shoulder, not even a shrug, really—a twitch. If she said no, that was it. Even if she said, *Is it really important to you?*, I'd end up not going. I could only go if she said, *Sure, of course, no problem.*

She took a deep breath and let it out, then managed a small smile. "I guess that would be fine."

"If you don't want me to . . ." I started. "If you need me to—"

"No," Mom said. "It'll work out. I just . . . Quinn, you really have to clean up your whole room ahead of time. Everything has to be gone."

"Gone?"

"You know what I mean. I can't—"

"I'll make it look like Allison's," I promised.

"Well, you don't have to get carried away." Mom kissed me on my forehead. "You're the best."

I ran up the back stairs and started right in on cleaning.

I actually did load up a big bag to give to charity and another for garbage before I got distracted by *The Remains of the Day*, a book I love and hadn't reread recently.

I looked up, startled out of the old English manor I was in, in my imagination, and back to the bright white room that looked vaguely familiar, to see four bare legs in front of my slowly adjusting eyes.

"Quinn!" Phoebe said.

"Yeah," I answered, blinking. Allison was grimacing beside Phoebe, looking longingly back out my door. "Hey," I said as nicely as I could, folding down my page, forcing a small smile. "What's up?"

"I think we need a conference," Phoebe said, and pointed at my closet.

I stood up fast. As much as I deserved whatever Allison wanted to dish out, and as much as, to be fair, she is such a drama queen and makes Armageddon out of one poorly placed, never-should've-happened kiss, I still was beyond shocked that she was bringing in Phoebe—Phoebe!—to continue harassing me over it. Fight your own battles, you know?

That's what I was thinking as I held open my closet door and let my sisters precede me into my huge closet. Allison refused to look at me as she passed me. Following them in, I told myself to just sit there and take it, not defend myself. Whatever Phoebe had to add to what Allison had said to me and about me earlier couldn't really hurt that much more, and was nothing in comparison to what I thought of myself, anyway.

I sat down on a pile of my old crap and waited for the onslaught to begin.

"Here's what I think," Phoebe said.

Allison and I glowered, our jaws clenched as tight as our fists.

"They're really sad, and we need to do something to cheer them up."

"Who?" Allison asked.

"Mom and Dad," Phoebe said. "Duh. Who did you think?"

Allison shrugged.

"So I had an idea," Phoebe continued, leaning forward and whispering. "I'm not sure if we can manage, but maybe if we work together we could get it up before they get home."

"What the hell are you talking about?" Allison asked.

"The piano," Phoebe said, exasperated, rolling her eyes at me like, *Isn't Allison so thick?* But I think I looked just as confused as Allison did.

I slowly explained to her, "Phoebe, they took the piano away. It's gone. They bought it on credit, and when Mom—"

"I'm not a mental defective, Quinn," Phoebe said.

"The other piano. The little one. The . . . uptight one."

"Upright," I corrected, before I could stop myself.

"Exactly," Phoebe said.

"Wait." Allison yanked Phoebe by the knee. "Quinn didn't get you to call this meeting?"

"No!" I yelled. "I thought you told her—"

"I didn't tell her anything!" Allison yelled back. "You think I'm such a—"

"But then why did she—"

"Hello!" Phoebe held up her hands in front of our faces. "I am still here; remember me? Nobody told me to call this meeting. I am a person here, not a puppet, not a toddler. It was *my* idea, and if you two can't stop bickering over whatever petty nonsense for long enough to do a nice thing for our parents, who are, hello, going through the worst time of their life right now, well, fine. I'll get some friends to come over and help me instead."

"No," Allison and I said at the same time.

Our eyes met.

"Jinx," Allison muttered. All three of us squelched unwanted smiles. Five years ago, maybe more, Allison went through this annoying phase where she loved to say *jinx* to people, mostly me, and swore I was absolutely not allowed to talk until she said my full name. I usually didn't even realize we'd said the same thing simultaneously until after she'd triumphantly yelled, "Jinx!" and then said my whole name and waited impatiently for me to thank her.

I remembered, suddenly, how annoyed I'd get. I wouldn't thank her because jinx was such a stupid, nonsensical game, and she'd accuse me of being no fun at all, and then for a while refuse to say my name after jinx, as punishment. I just went ahead and talked anyway, which drove her nuts. She'd have a huge blowout tantrum over it, and I would walk away sighing and shaking my head about what an impossible, immature jerk she was—but never thinking, *What's the big deal?* Why couldn't I go along with it, wait the half second for her to say my name, then say thank you and smile at her? It's just a silly game, true—but who was making the big stinking deal about it?

She looked at me, waiting for me to talk. So did Phoebe.

I mouthed the words, *Say my name!*

Allison closed her eyes. When she opened them again she picked up an old stuffed lion from my closet floor and twined her fingers into his mane. We sat there together in silence for a while.

Allison dropped the lion. "Quinn Miranda Avery," she whispered.

"Thank you," I whispered back.

The tears that came dripping down my cheeks surprised me.

"You're welcome," Allison answered, and when I looked up I saw a tear making a track down her cheek, too.

"Can somebody tell me what just happened?" Phoebe asked.

Allison and I both chuckled.

"Nothing," Allison said, and sniffed. "You are absolutely right, Phoebe."

"About what?"

"That we have our heads up our butts," I said. "Let's try to get that piano up. It's a great idea."

Phoebe looked warily back and forth between me and Allison. "What did I miss?" she asked as we filed out of the closet.

"Nothing," Allison and I both said, and for the first time ever, I said *jinx* first. She crossed her arms and waited. I pretended to be thinking over my options. Just as Phoebe was opening her mouth to say Allison's name, I said it in a rush: "Allison Beatrix Avery."

"You guys are freaks," Phoebe said.

We spent the next hour or maybe two cursing, breaking all our nails, smashing my pinkie toe and Allison's hip, chipping a hunk of paint off the basement banister, learning some new, shockingly obscene expressions from Allison, and, finally, placing the upright piano in the center of the living room.

It looked tiny in there.

"Should we put it against the wall?" Phoebe asked. "It looks kind of fragile like that—doesn't it?"

We stood back and looked, the three of us in a clump.

"I think it looks kind of . . . defiant," I said.

"Yeah," Allison agreed. "Fierce."

"Yeah," Phoebe said. "I guess. Like, 'Okay, I'm way small for the job, but I'm still here, damn it.'"

"Yeah," I said. "It looks like an Avery."

When Mom and Dad got home, they saw the note we'd left in the kitchen saying they should go to the living room. We were hiding on the steps as they headed there, note in hand, wondering aloud what the heck we'd done. They didn't glance up to see us peeking down at them as they passed us.

They didn't make a sound after they rounded the corner into the living room. We waited. Nothing. We glanced at one another from the corners of our eyes, waited, shrugged, and finally tiptoed in to see what they were doing.

Mom's hands were up at her mouth. Dad's mouth was hanging open and he was blinking up at the ceiling as he reached for Mom with his long grappling arm and drew her toward him. As she curled into his chest, we saw her see us, but before she could say anything to or about us, Dad said, "We are rich beyond measure."

"Yes," she whispered. "Yes, we are."

The three of us tiptoed upstairs to leave them alone there. Allison gave Phoebe a hug and whispered good night to her, but wouldn't even look in my direction. I didn't push it. We each went to our own rooms, but we closed the doors soundlessly, gently. We fell asleep to the tinkling, familiar sounds of "Summertime" being played on our old not-at-all uptight piano.

As I slept I was having a dream of being the soloist, marooned on a piano bench between an orchestra on my left and a huge, oceanic audience on my right. There was no sheet music on the piano and I had no idea what I was supposed to be playing. I was in a long black dress, my hair blown out and hanging long and straight down my back (though when I actually perform I always wear it in a bun), and, peeking out from under the dress, toes on the pedal, my feet were in my mother's fuchsia stilettos, the ones I had taken and hidden in my underwear drawer. I got distracted by them in the dream, maybe—I don't know, but anyway, I was sitting there at the piano, clueless and frozen, as the conductor tapped his baton on his stand and glared at me.

Tap, tap.

Tap, tap.

Tap, tap.

I opened my eyes. *Tap, tap, tap, tap.* It was Allison. She was outside my window, clinging to the ledge so she wouldn't fall off the roof into the bushes below, and mouthing my name.

I pushed the window open. "What the . . ."

"Jeez, Quinn, how heavily do you sleep? I've been out there for . . . How long have we been tapping?"

166

She turned around to ask it as she climbed over me, and coming in through my window, onto my bed, was Tyler Moss.

"Five minutes at least," he said. "Hi, Quinn."

I blinked a few times, trying to figure out if one dream had interrupted another.

Allison grinned and lifted her finger to her lips. "Shhh. Go back to sleep."

She grabbed Tyler's hand and started across my room.

He smiled sheepishly at me. "Excellent window."

My mouth dropped open.

"No way," I whispered. "Allison!"

She turned around and glared at me, her hands on her narrow hips.

Tyler turned to Allison and whispered, "She's right. I'm past curfew already. My dad's on the warpath as it is. I should go." He reeled her in and they made out, standing in the middle of my rug, as if I weren't a couple feet away in my bed, watching them like an insomniac kid with one of *those* channels playing on her TV.

"Hello," I said.

Tyler ran his hand across Allison's choppy hair and traced the line of her jaw with his fingers. "Night," he said.

He was crawling across my bed when Allison answered, "Night."

I dropped my head into my hands. "Go!"

I didn't lift my head, but his wicked grin was unmissable anyway. "See ya," he whispered as he backed through my window. I shut it behind him.

I turned to Allison, who was for once just smiling, so happy and relaxed, not talking, not arguing, not defending herself or tearing herself to bits.

"Good night," I whispered.

"Yeah," she said, and drifted out of my room the other way, toward the hall and her room beyond.

"Hey, Al?"

She turned around.

"I'm really sorry," I said. "About . . . you know. I was just . . . It didn't mean—"

"Okay," she said. "Everybody is a sleaze sometimes. Even you, apparently."

I nodded. "Thanks, Allison."

She turned around slowly and floated toward her room. I lay back down in my bed and fell asleep looking at my window, soon to not be my window anymore, imagining sand emptying out of a cosmic hourglass for somebody someday to climb up for *me*.

19

I GRABBED MOM'S SHOES and skipped barefoot out the door to wait for Oliver outside. I didn't want him to have to decide whether to ring the doorbell or honk his horn, didn't want him to have to come in and face my parents and sisters. I wanted to be outside, a light breeze whispering through my hair, reading a book on the bench at the top of the driveway and then, when he pulled up, I'd lift my eyes from the page, and he'd smile and look into me with those eyes of his. . . .

I knew it wasn't a date. I just wore Mom's shoes to please myself.

I had sworn to myself, to my parents and sisters and both Jelly and Adriana all week, that it wasn't a date.

But on some level I guess I kind of thought it was a date.

Which was why it sucked so horribly much when Oliver pulled up with a beautiful girl sitting in the front passenger seat. I climbed into the backseat, where another couple was sitting. They made room for me. Oliver introduced me to them and I forgot all three names instantly, maliciously. *I don't care,* I was thinking. I didn't want to look like a petulant toddler, but when Oliver tried to include me in the conversation the most I could manage was, "Yeah," or, "I dunno." Eventually he gave up.

I squished as tight as I could against the door and did my best imitation of not existing, despite my sparkly shoes, the whole ride and after, as we parked, then wandered into a beautiful park. We spread out the blankets they'd brought, and the picnic Oliver had packed; I barely said a word. They poured wine in a plastic cup for me. I took a sip but it felt like liquid fire going down, so I surreptitiously poured it out, drop by drop, into the grass when they weren't looking at me (which was basically at all times). My head felt hot and then kind of swimmy as the concert started, and then I got really chilled, despite the little black cardigan I had stolen from Phoebe's closet to wear over my tight blue tank top. I had thought, with my tightest jeans and Mom's stilettos, that I looked kind of cool, funky, a little older, like maybe nobody would think, *Is that guy babysitting that little girl?* Instead they'd think something like, *Hot young couple.*

If anybody at the concert thought anything of me, it was probably that one of those four cool-looking, funky, college-age, laughing, flirting, happy people had been forced to bring along the cranky little sister, bummer.

Oliver glanced over at me but said nothing, then slid his eyes away, back to the Girl, and laughed at some dumb thing she said. The depth of my hatred of my life right then had never in history been plumbed.

Eventually, maybe midway through the concert, it became clear to me that I was actually getting sick, not just from embarrassment or disappointment but also truly, legitimately sick.

I put my head down on the blanket and closed my eyes to listen to the music, trying to block out the quiet murmurs of the two couples on the blanket with me. I didn't want to see the girl whose slim, hard body tilted toward, then leaned against Oliver in the dimming light of dusk, as he whispered into her delicate ear with its dangly earring. I had no interest in looking at her wavy black hair, her black-rimmed eyes, her cute white shirt with the pretty little buttons down the front, unbuttoned to let her tan skin and pink camisole peek out the top, her platform sandals kicked off and toppled right in front of my eyes. I closed them (my eyes) and tried to think, *It doesn't matter,* but what I actually was thinking, horrifyingly, inappropriately, was *I want my mom.*

I want her to come get me. I want her to show up here at the concert and tower over this blanket and have us all look up at her, stronger, more beautiful, more powerful and brilliant than any of us, and she'd be looking only at me. I want to stand up and let Mom wrap her arms around me and bring me home. I want her to carry me up to my room and then to sit on the side of my bed and push my hair off my sticky, steamy forehead with a damp but not wet, warm but not hot washcloth and sing me the "okay" song she made up for me when I was a baby, which goes:

Okay, okay, okay, okay, okay
Okay, okay, okay, okay, okay

And makes me feel taken care of and loved.
I want to go home.

Well, that was the crappiest thing I could possibly have thought, that word: *home. I want to go home? Yeah, well* (came the nasty voice in my crushing skull, drowning out the music), *good luck to you, because you can't go home; you are stuck here with these strangers who don't really know you or love you or even care about you at all, and you'd better get used to it because this is just a metaphor for life. You are alone. Everybody is a stranger. Soon you'll head off for college anyway, and after that, a series of anonymous apartments, probably, and you will be an adult. This is called growing up, dork. Only a baby whines, "I want to go home." Grow up. The house you picture when you think the word* home *is just a house, a house your family basically no longer owns, a borrowed, temporary house that some other poor, deluded kid will picture when she (or he) hears the word* home, *until she (or he) learns the truth:*

You are alone, and there is no such thing as home. It is a made-up concept, an illusion. Get over it, you naughty kitten.

That's when I knew I had a fever.

That terrifying (trust me, terrifying) phrase is from a picture book Mom bought and read to me when I had a really high fever in kindergarten. In it three adorable little kittens are warned by their mother not to lose their mittens, because if they do, they'll have no pie. And then they do, of course, lose their mittens, and their harsh cat mother says, "You naughty kittens! You lost your mittens! Now you shall have no pie!" At the end I think the kittens manage to find their mittens and the mom is satisfied enough to tell them, "Now you shall have some pie." I hated that book. So horrible! Partly it was wondering why the kittens even had mittens (just because they rhymed? Why didn't the mom cat have a hat, then?), and why, if the mom was so worried they'd lose them, she sent them outside wearing them, and then I couldn't help wondering if the kittens even liked pie. I didn't. I did, however, tend to lose my mittens.

I knew which of the kittens in the book was me (the one who always went first, no smile, serious), and which was Allison (wide-spaced eyes), and which was Phoebe (the littlest, the cutest). It was so obvious, it never occurred to me that the kittens might *not* represent us.

Nobody knew I hated that book. I didn't want Mom to think I was wimpy (who is scared of a picture book?)

173

or ungrateful, a complainer, for fear that maybe she'd say, "You naughty kitten, you don't like this excellent book that your loving mother is so generously reading to you instead of doing the million things she needs to do! Now you shall have no pie!" And despite my abhorrence of pie, I would cry if she ever talked to me that way, the way I knew she might if I did the wrong thing. If I messed up someday that's what would happen—it was always looming out there; maybe the book had been bought as a warning? I remember lying there at five years old in her bed, all fever-ish and sweating, thinking maybe she had read me that book because she wanted me to know that if and when it happened, if I disappointed her, if I messed up, she would look at me that way, talk to me in that horribly disgusted, shaming voice.

And then I would disintegrate into crumbs and blow away.

Since that day, I have been on constant guard against bringing out that *you shall have no pie* Mom, the one who talked to Allison that way so often, the one I knew was one mess-up away for me. Allison could handle it, somehow. I knew that I couldn't. Mom's disappointment in me would destroy me. I knew it all the time but could shove it out of my mind unless I cooked up a fever.

I managed not to puke on the way back to the car after the concert ended. The pretty girl was no longer draped on Oliver, who looked like he was in a foul mood himself.

We piled into the car. Oliver, surprising me, put in an Elvis Costello CD and it blasted the whole way. I think I fell asleep, because the guy beside me was gently shaking my shoulder the next thing I knew. I pried my eyes open.

"You're home," he said.

"Ha, ha, ha," I responded, and stumbled out of the car. Oliver didn't even say good night, and neither did I. He backed fast down the driveway.

All I could focus on was *Do not puke on Mom's shoes*. After I finished my barf-fest into the hydrangeas, I went in the mudroom door.

"I'm home," I called, kicking off the shoes and hiding them behind my suddenly clammy back, just in case anybody barreled into the mudroom to greet me.

And then I cried, not just because on their way behind my back the shoes had revealed mud stains halfway up their heels, and Gosia, who had said that dirt stains are almost impossible to remove but would have helped me try, was gone forever. It wasn't even just because of that whole "I'm home" thing. I was crying, weeping really, because nobody else was home; I was alone, and cold, and sick, and shivering, with impossible-to-fix muddy stolen shoes and no mittens at all.

20

I SPENT THE NIGHT WAKING up sweating, shivering, wishing somebody would come. Nobody did.

I thought I'd barely slept but apparently I did, because I missed all the drama. As usual, where there's drama, there's Allison. She and Tyler had the brilliant idea to mess around out by the pool after she came home and said good night to Mom and Dad, who had gotten home sometime after me but before her. She went to her room, but then when she thought everybody was asleep, she slipped down the back stairs and out the back door and found Tyler, who was waiting for her on the double lounger. I don't know what they were doing (don't want to know, thanks very much), but whatever it was, it was sufficiently loud to rouse Mom and Dad, who showed up in the backyard, looming over the two young lovers, who eventually noticed they were no longer alone on the pool deck.

I did vaguely hear some yelling, which must have

happened after Tyler Moss, removed clothing in hand, had already been dispatched and Allison had been dragged, yelling and cursing their "rudeness," into the house. I incorporated it into my dream, which had me playing piano in a concert. Oliver was conducting but also making out with his slinky slut girlfriend, and Allison was screaming from the audience because nobody was paying attention to her for once.

Then in the morning the phone rang. Mom and Dad had to run out and pick up Phoebe, who had hurt herself on her friend's trampoline at her sleepover party. They left in a hurry to pick her up and take her to the emergency room.

I took the opportunity to grab Mom's shoes from where I'd hidden them under a pile of my junk, to return them. There was caked dirt up the heels and some mystery stains near the toe of the right shoe. I did my best to clean them but Gosia was right. They were the bad kind of cleaned up, the kind like somebody had messed them up and noticed—noticed enough to try to clean them but failed.

There was nothing more I could do, though. I decided to put them back in Mom's closet, behind some others, in a box. With any luck, it would be a long time before she noticed them and she might think she had messed them up herself. I was on my way out of my room right when Allison burst out of hers. We stopped and stared at each other. I tried to let the shoes dangle inconspicuously from my fingers while Allison raged about the torment of having our parents as parents. She was well into her fourth paragraph of complaints when she stopped suddenly.

"What's with you? You look like puke on toast."

"Urgh," I said. The last thing a person who is trying not to puke needs to hear is the word *puke*.

"Are you hungover?" she asked incredulously.

"No," I moaned. "Sick."

"And what are you doing with Mom's shoes?"

I dashed back into my room and ran for the bathroom; I was unable to hold in the puke any longer.

"Ew," I heard her say, out in the hallway. "Phoebe? Where's Phoebe?"

I couldn't interrupt my barfing long enough to tell Allison where Phoebe was. I clutched the cold porcelain and waited for my body to finish turning itself inside out. In the five-minute postpuke grace period of feeling able to stand upright, I brushed my teeth, washed my face with a cool, damp-but-not-wet cloth, then went to my room, changed into my coziest pajamas, and got back into bed. When I noticed Mom's shoes displayed garishly in the middle of my floor, I had to force myself up long enough to toss them into my closet.

Mom, Dad, and Phoebe got home sometime later in the day. Phoebe had a torn tendon in her left ankle with a pink cast on it, and crutches. After they settled her in on the couch with pillows and a movie to watch and a cool drink to sip with a straw, over her protestations that she was fine, fine, Mom and Dad got back to the business at hand, which was, of course, dealing with Allison.

Meaning: yelling at her, demanding explanations, voicing their disappointment. I fell asleep listening. It was as much my lullaby as "Summertime," listening to the same old tune of my parents (mostly, honestly, my mother) yelling at Allison.

In my dream, I saw Gosia looming above me, holding Mom's messed-up shoes like a sinister mobile above my face, and saying in a harsher voice than she'd ever used in real life, *"Dirt stains are almost impossible to remove. Dirt stains are almost impossible to remove. Dirt stains are almost impossible to remove."*

The next time I woke up, Mom was in my room asking, "Why are you in bed?"

"Um, I'm sick," I said.

She felt my forehead. "You're not hot."

"I was," I said.

"Hmm," she said. "Well, I'm glad you're feeling better."

I'm not, I thought but didn't say.

"I have to run out," she said. "Can you listen for Phoebe? She isn't used to the crutches yet, so if she needs anything, will you help her?"

"Okay," I said, then, "Mom?" But she was already gone.

The next morning, Monday, I still felt crappy, and way too weak to handle camp. I wandered down to the kitchen. Mom was there, back from her run, drinking a tall glass of water. "Hiya, sweetie," she said.

"Hi."

"Everything okay?"

"I'm still sick," I said.

"Really? Well, can you rally and go to camp?"

"I don't think so," I whispered.

"Oooh." She put her glass in the sink. "You'd better call Jelly and let her know not to come get you, then."

"I'm on it, Mom," I snapped at her. As if I suddenly needed her, after she'd been largely absent, working these past few years, to barge back into my life and tell me when I had to call my best friend? *Thanks, anyway, Mom. You are too late.*

"You are so good," she said, oblivious, kissing my forehead. "You don't have a fever. Sore throat?"

"No," I said, my teeth clenched against the stream of bile that might come pouring out at her.

"Headache? Period?"

"Just . . . sick." *Sick of you, sick of myself, sick.*

"Lousy." She bent down and untied her laces to slip off her running shoes. "Wish I could stay home and play hooky with you, take a girls' day, mental-health day."

I shrugged. She had no job; why couldn't she?

"Can you keep a secret?" she asked me, her eyes glinting. If she were my age, she'd totally be in with the social crowd, with every crowd. She's perfect. Adriana would adore her instantly. Oliver and his funky friends would crowd around her, attracted to her obvious brilliance, if she were eighteen, or even sixteen; beyond her achievements, she'd just know how to be. A torrent of nasty epithets flooded my brain.

"Yeah, of course," I assured her instead.

"I have a meeting today, lunch. I have a really good feeling about it. I think . . . I really think we're going to get this all settled, come to terms. Knock wood." She banged against the pantry cabinet, which she never does; only Grandma knocks wood. Weird. "There's no reason it shouldn't work. It benefits everybody."

I could smell the fire, but I blinked away the memory of her burning her papers. "You mean they might not sue you? The lawsuit might just get settled?"

She knocked the cabinet again.

"So you'll just get off, just like that?"

"We shall see," she said. "It takes a lot of work to get lucky."

It wasn't that I wanted her to get caught, or go to jail, or be punished in any way. I was just struggling to put together what I had seen and the possibility that it might just all turn out fine and life could resume, as if she'd never done anything wrong but remained as flawless as I'd imagined her to be, wished she could be. As if nothing had happened, we could all just blithely move on.

I met her sparkly eyes. "So we might not have to . . ."

"To what?"

"To move?"

"Oh, no," she said, yanking her ponytail holder out. "We have to move. We lost the house, lost the mortgage. But on we go, right? No failures, just temporary setbacks. We're strong; we're invincible. We are the Avery Women."

"Yeah," I said, leaning against the counter, because, despite my status as an Avery Woman and therefore strong, invincible, etc., I was actually so far from all that. I was still sick and hadn't eaten in two days and was therefore a bit wobbly, on top of everything else.

"So wish me luck," she said on her way out of the kitchen, her running shoes dangling from her fingers the way her shoes had dangled so recently from mine. "And hold down the fort, will you? Your sisters are falling to pieces. Good thing I can count on you!"

I think she blew a kiss at me. I couldn't be sure, because I had sunk down to the floor against the refrigerator by then.

Mom and Dad went out for a walk together Monday night after dinner, to discuss the Settlement. She was taut again, distracted and shiny, which was reassuring, kind of,

182

though she was also a little more jittery than usual. Phoebe was still on the couch and Allison was texting like mad, when she looked up and asked me how long I realistically thought they'd be gone.

"Don't even think about it," I said.

"You are such a prig," Allison snapped. "It's like I have three parents."

"Shut up," I shouted. She and Phoebe stared at me.

I went upstairs and took a shower, because I decided I was absolutely going back to camp again Tuesday. I still felt pretty woozy and had developed a really attractive cough (one that sounded weirdly like my great-uncle Alton's, the guy with the chewed-up cigar permanently dangling), but the thought of another day fetching Phoebe lemonades and smoothies, and listening to what control freaks our parents were for grounding Allison the lunatic slut attention hog— when next weekend was going to be the best party ever with the best people ever and if they forced her to miss it they may as well drive a stake through her eye because her life was basically ruined—was more than I could handle.

Adriana and Jelly spent the whole next day, between dealing with relay-race day and the skinned knees it engendered, talking about the amazing party coming up over the weekend. In my weakened state it took me five full minutes to put together that it was the same amazing party my sister had been talking about.

"You have to come with us," Adriana said.

Us, I noted. Adriana and Jelly had become *us?*

"It's gonna be sick!" Jelly said. "Speaking of which, what happened to you? Did you get wrecked with Piano Man Saturday night or what?"

She was clearly trying again to be light and fizzy Jelly. The strain showed in the corners of her eyes, and I loved her more than ever for it.

"Wrecked," I mumbled. I told them what had happened, despite the fact that I am a pretty private person, particularly when it comes to stories that make me seem like a complete and utter dork. I guess I was feeling a little . . . I don't know . . . needy.

They both hugged me and said mean things about Oliver, and meaner things about his skanky girlfriend and their pretentious loser friends. We walked around with arms linked much of the day. They made me laugh, and they made me feel like a funny, hot girl instead of a loser little kid slinking home with her tail between her legs.

An hour later, though, I felt this pit of self-loathing start to spread through my belly. It felt like I had sold out my complex, complicated feelings about Oliver for the chump change of their burbling comfort, and for the hedge against being left out of their suddenly chummy companionship. I had made Oliver sound like a typical two-dimensional bad-date jerk, made them hate him so that I could feel like less of a loser, and less alone.

Nothing is sacred to me, I scolded myself. *Allison is right about what a small, envious girl I am.*

And still I couldn't help enjoying and appreciating the camaraderie Adriana and Jelly were showering on me all day. It wasn't praise for high achievement or awe at my amazing abilities they wanted to crowd near. It was just fellowship, and it felt really good.

And at the end of the day, when I was feeling pretty bucked up, I said absolutely I'd go to the "sick" party with them. Jelly reminded me we'd have to get out of Ziva's farewell bash. "No problem," I told her. "It'll be a nerd-fest anyway."

"Yeah," Jelly said. "I guess that's true."

Adriana laughed like I was hilarious and suggested that maybe I could deep-condition my hair tonight. She mentioned "product" that was excellent for straight hair like mine and Jelly's. Jelly typed it into her BlackBerry and forwarded it to me. So we were all set, I guess.

Ramon slipped onto my lap during the singalong. We were all arrayed on the hill of the quad, and a breeze was blowing. It was a little less humid than it had been, and the sun had that hazy midsummer blur to it. Realizing I'd missed him the day before, I cuddled Ramon while we sang, "I want to walk"—*clap clap*—"a mile in your shoes . . ." (So different from songs we sang at my fancy sleepaway camp, which were all variations of the theme, *We are the blue team; let's kill the red team!*)

"You know what I want to be when I grow up?" Ramon

whispered to me, as the singing counselors started the next song, the one about the Hudson River.

"No," I whispered back. "What do you want to be?"

"Guess."

"Let's see. You're really smart, and sweet, and perceptive. A doctor?"

"No. Guess again."

"A teacher?"

"Getting warmer."

"A scientist? A writer? A lawyer? An astronaut?"

"No." His gappy smile stretched across his normally serious face.

"You can be anything you want to be, Ramon."

"I know," he said. "I want to be a counselor at this camp, and then we can get married."

I felt myself start, honestly, to blush. "You'll be an excellent counselor someday," I told him. "And an excellent husband, too."

He nodded. "I know. I would bring you flowers sometimes because that's what the ladies like."

The song about the Hudson ended and it was time to gather ourselves to go. "Well," I said to him, "if I don't get to be your wife, Ramon, some other girl is going to be so lucky."

"I already decided on you. But now I have to run around," he told me, in great seriousness. "It's a long bus ride home."

"Good thinking," I told him, and watched while he zoomed around in circles with his buddies, playing a more creative variation of the freeze-tag game Jelly and Adriana and I had taught them earlier in the summer.

I watched, smiling.

As we were getting into her car, Jelly got a text from JD. He wanted to meet her and hang out. She took a deep breath. "I should, right?" she asked me. "He's really cute, and he thinks I'm cute. So that's good. Right?"

"Sure," I said.

She texted back, *Yes*, with an enthusiastic emoticon, then threw her cell into the backseat. "Do you mind if we listen to classical?"

"Not at all," I said.

We drove home without talking, just listening to the music. When we got to the top of my driveway, Oliver was sitting on my front step.

"Uh-oh," Jelly said. "What does this mean?"

"I don't know," I whispered.

"You want me to stay or go?"

I swallowed hard and looked at my best friend. "Go, I think. Is that okay? You have a date with JD anyway."

"I'd cancel if you need me to. No problem."

"I know."

She nodded. "Mason totally asked where you were at the party we went to Saturday."

"Thanks," I said.

"Keep that in your head, okay?"

I unbuckled my seat belt. "I will. Thanks." I opened the car door. Oliver was staring at us still, his expression serious and sorrowful.

"And," Jelly said, grabbing me back, "more important: I know you better than any guy does. And I know you *are* better—better than any of them."

I shook my head. "Oh, Jelly. I'm so not." I closed the door and headed toward Oliver.

He kept his head down and waited until I sat down next to him before he started talking.

"I owe you an apology, Quinn."

I started to interrupt, but he held up his hand, so I shut up.

"I do. I just . . . it's been a weird year all the way around. I've changed, but people . . . my parents, my friends—it's invisible and of course self-centered to think the universe shifts just because something in me changed. But that's neither . . . Saturday was . . . I was an idiot."

"Why?" I asked. "What did you do?"

"Well, for one thing, I never should have involved you. I mean, you said it was fine, a group of us, you didn't mind, but still."

I did?

"The thing is, I met Cassandra a few weeks ago, and she's . . . well, obviously she's very beautiful, and we hit it off, and I was thinking this concert, here's a chance to, you know, raise my middle finger to the wisdom that said you couldn't go out one night and drink, listen to the Grateful Dead, and make out with a pretty girl and then turn around the next night and impress her with your love of Beethoven—the 'real' you. The real me."

The ground was spinning under me. "Ah," I managed, or possibly, *Ahhh* . . .

"Tickets for the Emerson String Quartet in the Spanish Courtyard," he continued, looking off into the middle distance. "It could hardly be better designed. One of the premier quartets in the world, performing outdoors on a perfect summer night, surrounded by maybe a hundred and fifty people, including the smartest, most amazing girl in the world—that's you, by the way. Damn it, screw me, I was using you, too—going to impress Cassandra by how cool our friendship is, yours and mine. How unlikely, sort of, and different, deep, and . . ."

He shook his head at his own perfidy. I was motionless.

"I guess I was sort of thinking about how you look at me, and *get* me . . . you know, maybe she would . . . I don't know. And the program—Shostakovich and Beethoven. How better to say to her that I am brilliant, among the elite, I grasp the highest things that man has endeavored to attain, or express. Oh, my God, could I be more of a self-aggrandizing jerk?"

"Hardly," I said.

A small chuckle escaped his mouth. "Right. Yeah, so there we were at the concert, and I was all, 'Yes!' The atmosphere, for starters; has there ever been such a perfect night? These incredibly gifted, insightful, devoted musicians, giving their all to one of the greatest works ever written, and afterward, with poor Cassandra . . . when she said, on the way back to the car, 'That was really nice.'"

"Nice?"

"I know. That's what sent me into that funk on the way home. But so unfair, really. It wasn't her fault. What did I want from her, from anybody?"

"I don't know," I said. "What did you want?"

He shrugged. "I guess to be admired, the way . . . well, the way you seem to admire me, maybe. To have her think highly of me because I had access to these things. I guess I wanted the reflected glory of it."

"Mmm," I managed, jaw clenched.

He dropped his head into his hands. "I am just too shallow for words. To trade on one's deepest calling so that a girl could be impressed and made more, whatever, willing . . . Urgh!"

"Oliver?"

"Yeah?"

"What the hell are you doing here?"

"What?"

"I think you should be apologizing to Cassandra, not me."

"Well," he said. "Of course, but I thought I owed—"

"I wasn't your date; she was," I said slowly. "I was just there to hold your mirror, Oliver. I'm the acolyte. You're right. I thought you were amazing. I always have. But you don't have to try so hard to impress me. I don't care that your professor thought you were brilliant. I like how you get my jokes, and how lightly your fingers hover above the piano keys before you start to play, the way you lean forward when you're listening. I have had a crush on you for as long as I can remember, which you have probably always known. Obviously you've enjoyed my worshiping you from afar. Well, that's good, because you know what? I'm done. I'm totally done. You're even hugely impressed with how petty you are. Could you stop evaluating yourself for one frigging second and just . . . be?"

"Quinn . . ."

"Welcome to the human race, Oliver Andreas," I continued, surprising myself at how fast the words were tumbling out, like they'd been packed under pressure until now, now that the lid was off. "We're petty and selfish. We are all unlovable, because we are all so messed up. I thought you were different."

"I'm not," he said.

"Okay. I was wrong. So thanks, Oliver, for setting me straight—and for setting me free from you."

I took a breath, finally, and looked at him. He was holding his head in his hands, just taking it. Good.

Softer, I said, "But you came to the wrong place, pal. I wasn't the one you were hoping to get into your bed; she was. So what the hell are you doing on *my* front steps?"

I stood up and went into the house, leaving him alone there. Even though all his self-loathing could have been plucked right from my own thoughts, my own heart, there is only so much intimacy belonging to somebody else that a girl can steal and imagine her own.

21

Two hours later, he texted me asking if we could talk.

I deleted it without answering.

An hour later Jelly texted me, asking what had happened. I texted her :(and asked how her date went with JD. She texted back the same :(.

I'm kind of done being fab, she texted.

Me too.

Kind of ready for a West Wing *marathon instead of a mad sick party this wknd . . .*

I smiled at my phone, so squat and solid in my hand, and typed, *Me too.*

I reread the good parts of *Pride and Prejudice* and was asleep before ten, then woke up early. I watched the dawn whiten the sky and took stock in the shower. Everything was kind of back to normal, really, except actually better. My silly crush was finished. I was a good girl, a nerd. So be it. I was moving out of this house into another, and then probably another. Okay, so there it was. Just bricks and wood, plaster and granite and stainless steel, too much anyway. I had a few good friends and good PSAT scores and my parents' approval. Not so bad, really. Overreaching just makes you fall on your butt. Time to play some Pictionary and stop both cursing and editing my vocabulary. Maybe being a good girl is a tight box to squeeze myself into, but I fit into it a lot better than into the wild-child box.

Everybody probably gets cramped, no matter which box they end up in, right? I combed my hair and slicked it back into a ponytail, resolving not to be manically cheerful, but just a somewhat nerdy, good role model for my sweet campers, who deserved more of my attention than they'd been getting.

I double-bowed my sneakers and headed down to the kitchen.

Mom was already at the door, thumb-wrestling her BlackBerry, her wheelie suitcase standing at attention by her side.

"What's going on?" I asked her.

"What?" She didn't look up. "Hold on. Yes, what?"

"Where are you going?"

"Chicago," she told her BlackBerry.

"Did the settlement happen?" I asked her.

She smiled tightly without looking up from the tiny screen. "It's in the works. Looks good."

"So why are you going to Chicago?" I asked, aiming for a neutral delivery. *Everything is fine,* I reminded myself. "For the settlement?"

"New project."

"Are you, like, unfired? Rehired?"

"No," she said. "Urgh. Hold on. What? No. This is something else."

"Oh," I said. I waited for more, but she wasn't saying anything else. No *Can you keep a secret?* no *I can only tell you this, Quinn, because you are my number one, my favorite, my confidante.*

In the driveway, a car crunched over the gravel. "There's my ride," she said. "Hold down . . ."

". . . the fort," I finished for her, as she smoothly maneuvered her suitcase out the door. "I know. Mom? I really don't want to move. Is there any way . . ."

"Oh, Quinn," she said, once the phone was slipped into its holster and she freshly saw me there. "Shake it off. It's just a lot easier to sell a house that's more cleared out. Of all the stuff, the clutter." She shrugged her bony shoulder. "That's what the real estate agent says. So that's what we'll do. We'll just take what we need to your grandparents', put some stuff in storage. There's a stager coming. . . ."

"A what?"

"Daddy will explain. I have to run. You're the best! Love you!"

"Yeah?" I asked, but she was gone.

When I turned around, my father was there, behind me.

He smiled sadly. "A stager. See, we're learning a whole new vocabulary. She comes in and makes the house look great. Rearranges the furniture, takes some away, brings in stuff to make it look good, flowers, statues, mirrors. I don't know."

"A stager."

"Yeah. This is the way it's done. So. She's coming to take a look today. I'm going to have to rely on you a lot. . . ."

He said a bunch of other words: about how to decide which things would go into storage, color-coded labels for boxes, "think three months," "support your sisters, what with Phoebe being in a cast and Allison being Allison." I heard a few phrases through the buzz in my ears that was assaulting me at the same time: *It's really happening; we are losing our home we are kicked out we are homeless we are lost lost lost.*

"Are you okay?" Dad was asking. "Quinn? You feeling sick again?"

I managed to nod.

"Maybe it's the paint fumes," he suggested. "Or the lilacs."

"Yes," I said. "Does she ever . . ."

"What?"

"Listen?"

"Who?" Dad asked. "The stager? It's not . . . She's not decorating it for us; it has nothing to do with us, really. She just has a job to do; you can't—"

"Not her," I yelled. "Mom."

"Mom? Quinn, are you okay?"

"I don't know," I said, heading for the door, because Jelly's car was screeching up the driveway. On the way, I leaned my forehead against the cool of the stainless-steel refrigerator for a few seconds and then turned to look back at my father, his teakettle dripping in his hand as he regarded me with some level of concern.

"What's wrong, Zen?" he asked. "You look stressed. Is camp okay?"

"Camp is fine," I said. "I saw you. And her. Burning the papers that night. I saw. I know what she did."

"Quinn . . ."

"Don't," I said. "I know what I saw."

"She burned her notes, Quinn," Dad said. "She burned her own private notes—notes that could be taken out of context if this thing ever went to trial. Everybody has doubts, Quinn, everybody. But when they're written down and taken out of context, what is just thinking something through on paper, with all the pros and cons and worst-case scenarios—all that can sound like foreknowledge, and then decisions made can seem malicious instead of what they really are: a gamble that could have gone well but instead went the other way."

"I saw her," I repeated. "And I saw you. You were uncomfortable about it. Admit it, Dad. You make excuses for her after the fact, to me; you say you're not mad, you're proud and grateful and so supportive, the perfect husband, but you know she was wrong to do it. Bad. Criminal, maybe even."

"No, Quinn."

"Yes, Quinn," I yelled. "She walks around—and we all treat her—like she's some sort of god, but she's so not!"

"That's true, baby," he said, setting the teapot down, finally. "She's not a god."

"But you never get mad at her. You just appreciate her. Well, maybe you're the god around here."

He sighed. "I get mad, Quinn. I do. You're right. I try not to, but I get impatient, and it's true I would handle some things differently. I don't have all the answers, and neither does she. We're just muddling through, same as you, same as everybody. We're no different—"

"Exactly," I said. "But I thought we were. She said . . ."

"What?"

"The Avery Women," I said, swallowing back a ball of tears. "She's all like, 'We are the Avery Women. Nothing brings us down. We are special. We are never intimidated. We are so awesome.' But we're not; we're not different. We're just like anybody else. Nothing special. A bunch of petty, ordinary nobodies."

"I never said she was ordinary," Dad objected, coming toward me with his arms raised, like he could cuddle this rage out of me. "None of you—"

"No!" I banged the refrigerator with my fist. "I just . . . I don't get it."

"Get what?" Dad asked, stopping, leaning against the counter.

"How you can love someone so f . . . so flawed," I said.

"Flawed?"

"Yeah," I said, trying to stay calm but not fully succeeding. "Flawed. Because if you just love, no matter what, like it's not a choice, it's just . . . you get what you get—then so what, you know? You may as well love a stuffed animal, or a rock, or the person behind her in the supermarket line. But if you love somebody because she's great, because she's extraordinary and wonderful and irreplaceable—brilliant—and then it turns out she's not all that, in fact she's kind of ordinary and selfish and sometimes a jerk; then what? How do you keep loving her?"

"I don't know," Dad said. "You just do."

"Or," I said, "you just don't."

I let the door slam behind me as I left.

22

I WAS A SUBPAR ROLE MODEL yet again. I had so planned on being excellent at this job, but life had just sucked the spirit out of me.

Jelly told Adriana we couldn't come to the sick party with her, because we were going over to a friend's instead. Adriana just shrugged and said, "Whatever," and that we should text her if we changed our minds. She spent much of the day flirting with Rick, the swim god; Jelly and I kind of moped around together in her shadow.

That afternoon I came home to our partially staged, even less recognizable house, and instead of making myself head upstairs to pack up my room, I sat out back, my feet in the pool, spacing out.

Mom came home about an hour later, when my toes were pickled and my butt had fallen asleep. The meeting hadn't gone as well as she had expected, apparently; it was obvious from her slumping shoulders and the way she was barking orders at us to get going on straightening and purging the crap from our rooms if we didn't want her coming through the next day and throwing all our stuff out, but first could somebody help wrap the dishes and mugs? Allison stood on the counter and handed me dusty champagne glasses while Dad cooked up some rice and beans for dinner. By the time we sat down to eat Dad's old special comfort-food treat of Buried Treasure (beans, then rice, then melted cheese, fit to soothe the wild beast), Mom was muttering at everybody that we had a lot to pack, a lot to get done, and to stop asking her, "Where is the tape?" or "What should I do with this?"

"Can somebody else please be in charge of one damn thing, ever?" she demanded.

We brought our plates to the sink and then all steered clear of one another as we marched single file up the back stairway, clutching packing tape and color-coded tags. Allison slammed her door behind her. Phoebe's music went on as soon as she got into her room. I stood on the threshold of the white room formerly known as mine but now "staged" with a fresh white duvet with a pale pink double stripe marking the edge and a single pale pink rose in a bud vase on my dresser, where Vesuvian piles of papers and books had been when I left in the morning. I had no idea where all my stuff was and could not force my muscles to start looking.

So I did not do as I was told. I found my computer and

tiptoed to the guest room, and watched movies I downloaded pretty much at random.

That should have been my first hint I was en route to disaster.

Or maybe the hint was that I didn't get caught, didn't get yelled at; nobody lunged through the guest room door shouting, *Caught ya red-handed*. And that it felt kind of excellent, kind of like flying, to be doing something so wrong as sitting on the far side of the guest room bed, hiding, watching one movie after another while everybody else in my family worked. I felt wicked and free.

Once a girl has crawled out of her usual box, it is so hard for her to fit herself back into it. But a girl not in a box of any kind, it's sort of like being a turtle who shrugs free of her shell, right? How bad a plan is that? Where the heck do I find a new exoskeleton if I'm shedding the old one?

I watched some more movies to shut down weird questions and images like that. Then, after my eyes were dried out from staring without blinking at my computer screen, I did what I realized I'd been forcing myself not to do all these weeks:

I Googled my mother.

I closed my eyes for the fraction of a second it took for the page to fill with results, and then for a few seconds more. As long as my eyes were closed, I could still not know.

The first eleven results were all recent. Seven of them

were from the financial press, or blogs, and basically went over the same facts: She had invested more than she was allowed to of her clients' money in this stupid company she was sure had a huge new cancer-fighting drug in the pipeline. As the company's stock plummeted, she invested more and more—borrowed money, not her own, money she had no right to be plunging into the stock; she just kept shoveling it in. There were questions about how she did it. The SEC and the U.S. Attorney's Office and even, holy crap, the FBI weren't commenting.

I turned off the computer.

The FBI? Whoa.

That was in the *New York Times.*

So everybody knew. Everybody but me. No doubt my sisters had each already Googled her. What an idiot they must all think I was, what a self-deluding, naive fool.

I rested my head against the guest bed behind me and whispered the words I'd been holding back:

"I hate her."

She basically stole people's money, or at least mishandled it.

Okay, so she was either a crook or an incompetent.

Shit.

But it wasn't just what she did.

I was so sure she was innocent. So damn sure. It was so important to me that she was right, righteous. And she was just not.

My lower jaw was jutting out but I wasn't crying. I wasn't sad. I was pissed off. How could she do this to us? How could she fail this publicly, this big? I believed in her. I held her up to my friends, my sisters, and mostly to myself as this paragon of all that is good and admirable in a person. And she let me the hell down. How could she do this to me?

How could she even face herself? She walked around for so long all proud and confident, like she was all that, so wrapped in the stunningness of her success, it was almost blinding, when really she was just an ordinary failure.

At ten o'clock, I took a long shower in the guest bathroom. I blew-dry my hair, then lay down on the guest room bed and waited. Nobody came to say good night or check on me. At two a.m., I tiptoed around the house. Everybody was sleeping, looking so innocent. I stole a short skirt from Allison's closet and a red tank top from Phoebe's, then tiptoed into my parents' room.

They were jackknifed against each other, his arm seat-belting her, her hair wafting over his shoulder. I paused and watched for a moment, not sure if I was taking a mental image to save for some future I couldn't yet fathom or making sure they weren't about to jump up and catch me—or trying to imagine whether someday I would be sleeping in a big bed with somebody's arm seat-belting me.

When an eternity seemed to have passed, I tiptoed into

Mom's bathroom and surveyed her stuff. A tube of mascara and a red lipstick, palmed, came back out with me.

The next day at camp passed in kind of a blur. I still wasn't sure what I was going to do. After Ramon took the deep-water test and passed, he sat shivering next to me on the bench and asked what I was thinking about.

"About a guy named Schrödinger, who I read about."

"The guy from Peanuts? Charlie Brown's friend who likes Beethoven?"

I had to laugh. Maybe that was part of what had made me think of him, subconsciously. "No," I said. "A real guy. A scientist."

"What about him?"

"Well," I said, rubbing his arms to warm his skinny body up. "This guy Schrödinger said if he put a cat in a box with a poison thing that might or might not kill the cat, the cat is both alive and dead until you open the box and see how the cat's doing."

"No, it's not," Ramon said.

"The story is just to show that until you see what happens, every possible thing exists."

Ramon considered the theory all morning but by lunch had decided he still didn't buy it—Schrödinger's cat, in that box, was either dead or not dead, regardless of what Schrödinger thought or even hoped. "That's life, man," he said. "Your friend Schrödinger is not too smart. Plus, he has to face reality. Also, he should not be allowed to put cats in boxes, especially with poison. That's just whack."

"Can't argue with you there," I said, wiping the ketchup off his face.

"But," he added reassuringly, "I still think *you're* brilliant, Quinn."

"Thanks," I said, and went to get more bug juice for the thirsty campers.

Meanwhile, Adriana was laughing with other counselors. Jelly and I tried to smile at each other a few times before we gave up. She said she'd pick up a gift to bring to Ziva tomorrow from both of us, something good to bring to a journalism program, maybe pens or gummy erasers or gummy bears.

I said, "That sounds great—any of that, thanks."

My house, or the house I had been living in, looked quite lovely when I got home. It was clean and bright, with interesting art on the walls and no clutter anywhere, just botanical-garden-depleting masses of flowers in stunning crystal vases everywhere.

"No shoes!" a strange, tiny woman with huge lips and long highlighted hair barked at me.

I had the momentary thought that maybe I had accidentally wandered into the wrong house, or that this woman was a witch who knew telepathically that I had stolen and ruined my mother's shoes.

But no.

The shoes and the rest of the stuff I had stolen were

still hidden in an old duffel bag at the back of the top shelf of my mostly emptied vast closet.

Friday at camp, I barely said a word. Adriana was busy texting her real friends, and Jelly kept telling me about inside stuff, school and orchestra and people Adriana didn't know. Ramon was chosen second for T-ball and spent the day laughing with three other boys who had finally warmed up to him. I was mortified that in addition to being happy for him, I was a tiny bit jealous. On our drive home, Jelly said, "Adriana's not really as great as I thought—we thought—you know what I mean?"

"Nobody is," I said.

She nodded and we just let the Brahms on her stereo fill in the silence.

"See you tonight," she said as I got out of her car.

I watched her pull away and stood there alone, feeling the heavy humidity settle around me, thinking, *I am so stuck.*

A sudden breeze fluttered the leaves on the hedges and trees across our property. I watched their weird ballet. *Beautiful,* I thought. *I love it here. Loved it.*

"Home," I whispered, and like an answer the breeze doubled back and lifted my hair gently from my sweaty neck, a hint, a temptation of lightness. I closed my eyes and felt the cool relief. *Go,* the breeze was answering.

And for the first time all day, I smiled.

I didn't head downstairs until seven, makeup done and

bag in hand. I buttoned up my saggy white cardigan and asked Dad if he was ready to drive me over to Ziva's. He looked over at Mom.

I didn't.

"You're going out?" she asked me.

"You said I could," I heard my voice say, calm and steely, just like hers.

"Fine," she said. "We got an offer."

"On the house?"

She nodded. "Tentative. Pretty good. They're coming back tomorrow, measuring tapes and cameras. Are you almost finished with your room?"

"Yes," I said. "Almost."

"You didn't mess it up?"

"No."

"Great. You're the best."

"So I hear," I said.

"Could you buy more packing tape on your way back, Jed?" Mom asked him, turning back to the plates in a pile in front of her. I stood there and forced myself to look at her, kneeling in the midst of the small, contained mess within the vast polish of the kitchen we hadn't smudged by having dinner in. Nobody had even mentioned dinner, in fact, which was fine with me.

Her hair was tousled and limp, her forehead creased. She looked stressed, and small, and maybe even foolish, with a piece of packing tape stuck on the side of her

T-shirt, and sweat stains under her arms.

How had I never realized this was who she really was?

I didn't pity her. I just wanted to get out of there. I wanted to get away from her. I was almost finished with my room, yes, Mom. Almost.

I said no, thanks, to driving and slumped down in the passenger seat. I turned on alarmingly bad pop music and didn't chat with Dad on the way over to Ziva's, to avoid conversation.

"Packing sure is fun, huh?" he tried.

I shrugged.

"It's going to be hard to say good-bye to the house."

"It's just bricks and wood," I said.

"True," he remarked, easing away from a stop sign. "You are so wise, Quinn. What's important comes with us, right?"

"Sure. Whatever we can salvage of it." We pulled up in front of Ziva's house. It was small and cute, all one level, with a hanging plant blooming beside the front door.

"Have a good time, sweetheart."

"I will," I said, getting out.

He opened the passenger-side window and called, "Mom will pick you up at eleven?"

I nodded and walked up the crumbling slate steps toward Ziva's green-shuttered white wood house.

I stopped halfway up and waved good-bye to my father. When he was out of sight, I opened my bag and pulled out my cell phone and Mom's heels. Like Pandora, like Eve, I felt myself at the precipice, not deciding whether to make the move but holding my breath in anticipation of it.

Come get me, I texted to Adriana, and typed in Ziva's address. After I hit SEND, I went back down the stairs and walked to the curb, where I stowed my shoes and cardigan in Ziva's bushes. I slipped into my mother's fabulous shoes and waited.

23

THE PARTY WAS LOUD, HOT, and sticky. It smelled like beer and baby powder. The thumping music was more rhythm than melody, and none of the bodies crushed up against one another had been on the planet a full two decades. I chugged the first beer I was handed to dull my rising sense of panic at being there, then sipped the second one down to a level that stopped it from spilling out over my fingers as I maneuvered to keep up with Adriana. In my mother's shoes I was able to see above most of the girls' heads and many of the boys', too.

"Over here," Adriana said, her hand on my arm.

My beer was spilling but my head was pleasantly bubbly. I eased through the crowd in Adriana's slipstream until I found myself staring into a familiar face.

"Quinn."

"Hello, Ty."

"Is Allison here?"

"She's grounded," I said, eye-to-eye with him. "Because of you."

"Yeah, that sucked. You okay? You seem a little . . ."

"I am excellent," I told him. "No thanks to you."

He lowered his head and looked at me past his eyebrows. "Sorry. I thought you were going to tell her, and I . . ."

"Water under the tunnel," I said. I took another sip of my beer and laughed. "No, that's not it. Water under the . . . What is the water under?"

"Water?"

"Bridge," I said. "Or dam? Damn. No apologies. I am great. Tonight, I am excellent, in a whole different . . . Oh, but speaking of apologies, I've been meaning to . . . Sorry I kissed you that day."

"It's okay," he said.

"It must have been somewhat awkward for you."

"Yeah, somewhat," he said. "Not that . . . no offense. But I really like Allison, a lot, and . . ."

"I know," I said. "I do, too. It was just a weird day. I'm sorry."

"It's okay."

"I'm normally very shy."

"You definitely didn't seem shy," Ty said.

I laughed. The one guy ever who thought I was a hellion and he was in love with my sister. Figured. "I'm actually a pathologically good girl. Except that day. And tonight."

"Uh-oh," he said. "Tonight?"

"Quinn," Adriana called. "Come on!"

I gave a half shrug to Tyler and angled my shoulder to get past him. I watched his eyes look down my body all the way to the floor and then back up to meet my eyes. It was like we were dancing, slowly, as he backed up half a step to allow me to squeeze past.

"I'm . . ." I said, tottering a little.

He caught me by the elbow and said, "Excellent. Yeah, you said. Also, tall."

I laughed as I walked away from him. Yeah, dude, tall and excellent and fun. I could feel people's eyes on me, and I was in such a weirdly hot *screw you* happy mood, I liked it. I finished my beer just as I was catching up to Adriana, who had made it to the corner of the kitchen.

"Here she is," Adriana said. "I told you."

Mason turned around and looked at me. I met his blue eyes with my own. He was sexy; there was no denying that, and he knew it, too—you could see it in the way his broad shoulders rested easily across his spine, the way the edges of his mouth tipped slightly up as an indulged child's will at the sight of a new toy.

He handed me a red plastic cup full of cold beer. I took it and my fingers touched his.

Nobody said to me, *This isn't like you, Quinn.*

Nobody who knew me well enough to know that was there; nobody who knew me well enough to know that even knew where I was. I was a girl untethered. I was loose in the world, free. The people at the party thought this *was* me.

"Good to see you," Mason whispered into my hair, as his fingers touched my waist lightly enough to give me a shiver. "You look really hot."

I took a sip of the beer. The bitterness was gone; only the bubbly cold was left. It went down easily.

"Hello, Mason," I said.

I heard Adriana laugh a little, but I didn't flinch, didn't blush. I was feeling powerful and happy. Mason clinked his plastic cup against mine and mumbled, "To tonight."

"Tonight," I echoed, thinking, *This is actually more delicious than portcullis pretzels,* and took another sip of cold beer. Okay, maybe not better than. But I could still manage it. I could swallow it; I could.

"Quinn?"

I swallowed hard before I spun around, a calm smile on my wet lips.

"What are you doing here?" Allison demanded.

"I'm not grounded," I told her, my tongue a little lazy inside my mouth. "What are *you* doing here?"

"You're drunk!" Allison said.

I turned to Mason while throwing my arm around Allison's shoulders. "This is my little sister," I told him. "Allison. She's only fifteen. But she thinks . . . It's like I have three parents." I held up three fingers to illustrate my point. "She wants to kick me out of this party. What do you think?"

"I think you're both hot," Mason said slowly.

"Ew," said Allison. "Quinn, seriously. What's up? Dad said you were at the nerd-fest at Ziva's."

"And he said you were in the Tower of London," I told her, trying to make a joke, a historical reference, not sound like a priggish housewife or wannabe parent repeating that she was grounded. People didn't laugh along, though. Maybe British historical references were not the surest route to cool, after all. I laughed a tiny bit at my excellent sense of self-mocking humor.

"You are wasted," Allison said, and grabbed my arm. "Let's find Tyler and we'll get out of here."

Mason put his arm around me. "Not so fast, little sister," he said in his laconic drawl. "We're just getting reacquainted here."

He chugged his beer and pulled me close against his muscular chest.

"Hands off," Allison said to him, tugging at me.

"Allison!" I shook my arm out of her grip. "Lighten up, huh? It's a party."

"You've had enough," my crazy, wild sister told me.

"Not nearly," I answered, and started drinking my beer. I heard somebody whoop, so I kept going. *Oh, yeah,* I thought. *You thought . . . you all think that I am so good, so tame, so Quinn Avery predictable and good? You have no idea.*

I have no idea! I could be anything. I could be anybody.

I downed the last swallow and dropped my empty cup triumphantly on the floor, grinning at my sister, feeling Mason's fingers touch my hair. I was strong, powerful, sexy, wild. The faces around me were smiling, impressed, approving. The librarian takes down her bun, removes her glasses, reveals herself to be the sexiest woman in town. As I wiped my wet mouth with the back of my hand, I snarled at Allison, "I got some good advice recently, to stop pretending I was such a good girl. Excellent, excellent advice."

"You seem pretty good to me," Mason said, and after I kissed him, he added, "You taste good, too."

"Okay, that's it," Allison said. "Time to go, Quinn."

I yanked my rubbery arm out of her tight grasp. "Don't tell me what to do," I complained. "You're not my mother."

"Thank goodness," Allison said. "Because Mom would drag you out of here by the ear. Come on, boozer. Let's go home."

"Home?" I said. My voice was a little overloud, and I could sense people looking sideways at me, nervous, maybe not completely on my side anymore, but I didn't really care. "Home! Please. As if we had one. You mean that big, hulking shell of a place where our stuff currently is, half boxed up, crowded by bouquets of overpriced dalliances?" That made me laugh, it was so funny. "Not dalliances.

That would be . . . What would that look like? Bouquets of dalliances. I like that. What did I mean? Oh. Dahlias. Or lilies. In hopes that somebody would please buy our house already."

"Shut up, Quinn," Allison warned. "Come on."

"Oh, right, the defender of our family's honor and privacy," I said mockingly. "As if you have ever once done anything for our family."

"You have no idea what I've done," Allison hissed.

I smiled at Allison. "Right back at you, Al. You have no idea what I've done, either."

Ty was there, suddenly, beside her, his hands on her shoulders. "What's up? Everything okay?"

I got the giggles then. "Oh, wait," I said, as my ankle buckled. I clutched Mason to keep my balance. "That's right. Oops, you do know. Thanks a lot, Ty."

"She's wasted," Allison told Ty.

"I'm fine," I said, and spun around. "I'm excellent."

Partway around my spin, or it may have been at the one-and-a-half-spin mark, my face bumped into Mason's and then we were kissing. His face pressed hard against mine, and his arms wrapped around me. I was thankful for that, because the spinning had been a bad choice; I was feeling dizzy and unsure gyroscopically.

I pulled my mouth away and smiled at Mason. He smiled back, his eyes heavy lidded. "I'm like a sky-ro-jope," I said. "No, not that. I mean a gyroscope. Wow, I am having some serious word-retrieval issues tonight."

"Okay," Mason said, his face approaching mine again.

"Let's go," Adriana whispered into my ear.

"No," I said, without opening my eyes. "Why is everybody such a party pooper?"

"Now, Quinn," Adriana insisted.

"Why?" I asked, my mouth on Mason's. "Just go with Allison. She's more your type anyway, and she wants to go."

"Come on," I heard Adriana insisting, pulling me back. "The cops are here. We gotta go!"

"The what?" I had to close my right eye to see clearly. Mason kept his arm around my waist. "Let's go," he whispered. "It'll be okay. Come on."

Everybody was scrambling. I heard Allison calling my name, but I went the way I was being pulled. My heels (well, Mom's) were sinking into grass as my feet struggled to keep up with the top half of me. Then I was in a car, in the backseat, squished in the middle of a bunch of people, and everybody was laughing, including me, and then we were moving.

Fast.

The windows were open and the air felt good. Music was playing and wind was blowing and my friends and I were laughing. Adriana's head was on my shoulder, and she was singing way out of tune.

We were young and powerful and free; we'd gotten away, and through the open sunroof above my head the night sky was deep blue, moonless, full of stars.

I closed my eyes.

Mason's hands were all over me. I tried to swat them away but they were multiplying. "Come on," he was whispering in my ear. "Nobody can see."

I wasn't sure what that had to do with anything.

I tried to shift so my back would be toward him, but his hands snaked around front and his fingers were pressing, grabbing.

"I gotta get my . . . my phone," I said.

"Shh," Mason breathed, pulling me into him.

"I have to . . . have to call Jelly," I said, suddenly clutched by the powerful need to let her know where I was, so she wouldn't worry. A fast turn slammed me into Adriana.

"Don't call Peanut Butter," Adriana said.

"My bag is under your, urgh, foot," I said.

"She's . . . No offense," Adriana said, stretching her long neck so her head lay against the backseat but also on my shoulder. "Your friend Jelly is a bit of a tool."

"A bit?" somebody else said from the front seat, and I realized it was JD, driving. "She's a complete boring geek," he said, and sped up even more.

"No, she's not," I said.

"Oh, please," Adriana said.

"Maybe you shouldn't be driving," I whispered to JD. "Just take a break. . . ."

"Come on, bitty," said the guy in the other front seat. "Save the sermons, huh? Who is this girl, anyway?"

Mason got my button undone. I grabbed his hand and said, "Stop it." I shifted again so Adriana's head rolled off my shoulder, and when she lifted it to look at me through her thick, perfectly curled eyelashes, I said, "Listen, seriously. Jelly is the least boring . . . She plays all-county oboe and speaks three languages and went to the National Spelling Bee and raised over two thousand dollars for leukemia research and spends her Thursdays visiting her great-grandmother in a nursing home."

JD screeched to a stop at a red light. "Oh, man," he said. "She's more of a grind than I even thought!"

The light turned green and he peeled out.

"Fine," Adriana said. "She's great. Excellent résumé. I'd vote for her for president. But you were right about your sister. She's a real bitch."

"Don't talk about my sister."

"Mmm," Mason said. "Everybody stop talking." He yanked my head around and punched his mouth into mine.

"Get off me," I yelled, pushing his face away. My eyes were open and I sat up straight. I leaned forward between the front seats. I could see the headlights on the dark road ahead of us. We were not heading in a straight line, and we were going fast.

"JD, we need to pull over. Now."

"Whoa," Adriana said, with a cruel laugh. "You're actually kind of harsh, too, Q. What's the third one like? Scary crew. Wouldn't want to have dinner at your house, three bitchy daughters with your indicted-criminal mom and your sad little mousy dad."

It was like a door had closed. *Click.* Done. She had insulted my entire family in one sentence; it was almost impressive. I was speechless.

"Don't get mad," she purred. "I'm just saying, avoid dinnertime at the Avery house, or do you not have one anymore?"

"Shut up, Adriana," I seethed. "No worries. You're not invited."

"Oooh," she said. "I'm crushed. Serves me right, trying to do a good deed this summer, get a couple of desperate, résumé-pimping nerds laid."

"Screw you," I said, and leaned forward again, trying to speak calmly, reasonably. "I want to get out of this car now. JD, please stop the car and let me out."

"Relax," Adriana slurred. "Don't get your panties in a knot."

"Now!" I shouted. *"Now!"*

JD slammed on the brakes and swerved to the side of the road. Hands were on me, pushing me out. My shoe got caught on something and my bag wasn't budging but I was tumbling, pebbles scraping my knees and palms like a little kid falling off her scooter, and then I could taste dirt as pebbles hit me in the back, and the car I had been in screeched away with the door still open. I heard the laughter follow the car like a wake, until the door slammed. When the taillights disappeared around the corner, I was alone.

24

THE NIGHT WAS QUIET AND STILL.

I had no cell phone, no wallet, one shoe, and no idea where I was.

I stood crookedly, one leg propped four and a half inches higher than the other, courtesy of my mother's fabulous shoe, and breathed the night air.

Now what?

I looked both ways, up and down the street. Neither way seemed especially promising. After briefly considering sitting down on the curb and crying, I instead took off Mom's other shoe and stood on my bare feet on the patch of rough grass between the sidewalk and the street. I just stood there, waiting for some idea to come to me.

I'm alone, I thought. *I have never been this alone before.*

It's not metaphorical: I can't get home. I don't know how to get to where my home is from here. I am out somewhere all by myself, no way of contacting anybody, and nobody knows how to find me. Nobody can save me.

Not even Mom.

Not even my *Mom, who can do anything, who is not like the other moms, all small and petty, with their whiny, entitled voices and small concerns about junk food and screen time and PTA meetings. My mom, the colossus, the all-powerful, the world-shaking, sparkling center of everything, the most brilliant person I've ever met. She has no idea where I am. She can't save me.*

I looked up at the sky. "I'm here," I whispered.

I concentrated on the prickly grass under my toes, then the ache in my calves from having worn such high heels, the tightness in my left hip, the weight of Mom's shoe in my hand, the smell of beer and smoke clinging to my hair, the stale taste in my mouth, the crown of weight bearing down around the top of my head. I rebuttoned my button.

"I'm here," I said a little louder, to interrupt the silence, to test the possibility, or maybe the possible repercussions, of disturbing the night.

Okay, I thought. *I'm here. I don't want to be here, though. So.*

Go.

Which way?

I looked again up the street, down the other way. Houses behind lawns behind bushes as far as I could see in both directions, and darkness beyond, both ways.

One road diverged in a dark suburb, I thought.

And sorry I could not travel both

and be one traveler, long I stood . . .

Is that what I am? I wondered. *One traveler? With pieces of me scattered around town, in some guy's car, some guy whose last name I don't even know, or really his first name, only two letters and probably an emoticon* ☺. *My parents think I'm at a whole different place, think I'm a whole different person—how can these fragments add up to one traveler?*

I looked again up the road. Which way was less traveled? They looked about the same, as Robert Frost had observed in his yellow wood.

Choose, I told myself. *Just choose and go. Start walking. You'll end up someplace. And that will make all the difference.*

I turned left and started walking, my bare feet gripping the rough, scratchy earth.

It wasn't until I'd been walking for a while that I realized I hadn't cried, hadn't fallen apart, hadn't panicked or freaked out. I was in a pretty awful situation, the worst of my life. I had screwed up really badly. I was in huge trouble even if I managed to make it home unscathed by bad guys or worse. My parents were going to be shocked, and disappointed, and angrier than they'd ever been even at Allison. At me. And yet at this moment, I was handling the situation. I'd been drunk, yes, wasted maybe even, but I'd realized in the car that I had to get out, and I made them release me. Whether that was a smart decision or

225

not was still up in the air, but it seemed right to me; I was confident about it.

Great, I told myself, making a right turn at a corner, hoping I wasn't walking around in circles. *I'm competent. As expected. I don't panic in a crisis. Welcome back to the good-girl box.*

But no. That wasn't the whole of me. That girl at the party, that was me, too. Cinderella isn't a fraud at the ball just because she's in magic clothes. She's just as much herself there as scrubbing the fireplace.

Cinderella?

I wondered briefly if I was still drunk. No, pretty sober, I thought. Mostly, anyway. Then it hit me: of course Cinderella. I was wandering around sometime after midnight with only one shoe. Who else would I be?

I laughed out loud.

Yeah, so where the hell was Prince Charming, my other shoe in hand, to find me and restore me to my rightful place at the palace? To rescue me?

I stood at the next corner, holding the shoe, deciding which way to go again.

Straight.

I kept walking. I could damn well rescue myself, thanks very much.

I could find my own way home. If that's where I wanted to go.

Where do I want to go?

I recognized the house on the corner. The yellow house. Yes. I was someplace familiar. Okay, maybe not completely sober; my head was a little sloshy still. That yellow house is down the street from somebody's house I know. Whose?

I turned right and was already walking before I allowed myself to know whose house I was heading toward.

25

"OLIVER."

Nobody answered. Not that I expected him to hear me whisper his name from his driveway. I didn't even know which was his window. Was he supposed to just appear, like Juliet, up there?

I didn't try the front door but tiptoed around his small house, over the rough stones on the side, to the back. The screen door to their garden was closed but not locked. I slid it open silently.

Great, Quinn. Breaking and entering. Trespassing. You and your mom can rot in jail together.

No, no; she's not going to jail. She's getting out of it. She may not be innocent but she won't be found guilty. She's Settling the Case. It's all over the internet. She's Settling.

What a depressing word.

Who would want to Settle?

Not me.

Not me.

I don't want to settle. Not ever.

Anyway, I'm not breaking, I reminded myself, tiptoeing up the stairs to the bedrooms. *Just entering. They'd let me off for that, probably.*

Excellent morals, I praised myself.

Four closed doors off the upstairs hall. *Okay, now I'm "The Lady or the Tiger,"* I thought, and slapped my hand against my mouth to keep from laughing out loud. *This is not funny, Quinn! Sober up!*

Choose.

I reached for a doorknob and twisted it carefully. Not locked, at least. I pulled the door slowly open. My heart was pounding.

Okay, linen closet. The towels and sheets were mute witnesses to my trespass. I closed the door and tried the next. Bingo.

Tiptoeing across Oliver's wood floor, I held my breath. It smelled like boy in there, a little sweaty and dark. I knelt beside his bed and touched his dark, wavy hair and whispered his name again.

He turned over and his eyes flickered open. It took them a moment to focus on my face. Just when I thought he might jolt or scream, he gave me that half smile, half frown and said, "Quinn."

Like he wasn't shocked I had appeared in the middle of the night in his bedroom. Like his first thought was happy to see me.

I smiled back. "Hi."

He reached out and touched my hair and whispered, "You're here."

That seemed to wake him up. His eyebrows scrunched. "What are you doing here?"

I opened my mouth to tell him that it had been a crazy night, that I had wandered all over and come upon his house, or maybe I was heading here the whole time without knowing it, or at least without admitting it to myself, and my parents were probably going crazy-furious and that for the first time in my life I was furious right back; that my feet were cut and bruised and I was in deep trouble and I didn't know what to do. But I didn't.

Instead I leaned forward and kissed his lips.

To my surprise and delight, he kissed me back, his hand lightly touching my cheek. I knelt up higher. My eyes opened and looked into his, then closed again.

We pulled apart slowly, our breath swirling around each other's in the little space between us.

"Hold on," he whispered hoarsely.

I sat down on his floor while he threw back the covers. He was in boxer shorts. He grabbed a T-shirt off his dresser and went to his door, where he held out his hand to me.

I took his hand and followed him down the stairs, out the screen door to his backyard, across the garden, to the huge hemlock tree that dominated the yard.

He kissed me again. I dropped my mother's shoe.

Our arms wrapped around each other, our bodies pressed against each other's.

"Quinn Avery," he whispered.

"Yes," I answered.

"What am I going to do with you?"

"What do you want to do?"

He sucked in a big breath of air and let it out with a little chuckle. "I don't know," he said, serious now, and kissed me. His eyes were closed as he pulled slowly, gently, reluctantly away.

"Okay," I whispered. "You don't know. Excellent place to begin. Scary, maybe, but if you're brave enough to admit not knowing, you open yourself up to what might be. Does that make sense to you?"

"More than ever," he whispered.

"So, then, how does it make you feel?"

"Whole. Scared. Happy."

"And what does it make you think?"

"I think . . ." he started.

I kissed his neck, lightly, and heard him sigh.

"I think . . ." He kissed my lips, hard at first, and then so lightly it could have been his eyelashes against my lips. "Mmmm. I think I . . . I think you're in high school, Quinn."

"Not at the moment," I pointed out.

He laughed. "Good point." He kissed me again, then pulled away, groaning a bit.

"What?" I asked. "If you don't want to . . ."

"I want to," he said. "Quinn, please. I've wanted to kiss you all year. I come over every week to teach you piano and it's all I can do to keep my hands on the keys instead of on you."

"Really?"

His hand on my cheek. "Quinn Avery."

"You don't think I'm just some little kid who has a crush on you?"

"No." His lips were almost on mine. "No. You keep saying that, but it is so far from true. I wanted that to be what it was. But no. I think you are an intense, complex, shockingly sexy person, and I can't stop thinking about you."

Only his mouth on mine kept me from saying, *Seriously? Me? Brainy, geeky, good-girl me?*

He pulled away again. "But I also think I am in college and you are in high school, and there are rules against this." His fingers traced my collarbone. "Laws, in fact."

"Okay, Grandpa," I said.

"Don't."

"Okay, I won't, Grandpa."

"Quinn."

"You're what, two and a half years older than I am? When you're twenty-nine and I'm twenty-six, we'll be the same age. When you're eighty-four—"

"But not now," he interrupted. "You're not even seventeen, are you?"

"Almost. In one month."

"Almost," he said. "Urgh."

"And when we say what we think, you and I, it's like a fugue," I said. "Two voices, same melody."

"Yes," he said. "Oh, Quinn. I know." And he kissed me again. I touched his fingers with the skin of my neck, my back. "I'm so sorry, Quinn. I've been . . . All week . . . You were so right, and I deserved what you said. It made me realize what I've been trying so hard not to feel and . . ."

"Well," I said, touching his cheek as I looked him in the eyes, "my sister said everybody is a sleaze sometimes."

Oliver smiled his lopsided smile and closed his eyes.

"I miss your piano lessons," he said. "And not just the part about getting to be near you for half an hour."

"I do, too," I whispered. "I miss . . . I miss piano."

"You haven't been playing at all?"

I shook my head. "I miss it. I really . . . I wake up and my fingers ache from needing to play; I hear the music in my head all the time. . . . I mean, I know I'm not that great a piano player or anything. . . ."

"How do you know?"

"I wish I were. Maybe I should've switched to some other instrument, oboe, or . . ."

"Oboe?" His face looked so confused I had to laugh.

"No," I said. "Just . . . I . . . I know I'm smart. I'm

233

good at school. I'm good at piano, and taking tests, and writing an essay and following instructions. I'm a good girl. You know? But there have been teachers, and even my parents, who seem to think I could be, or am, brilliant. At something. And I can't figure out what at." I hiccuped. "Excuse me."

"You're excused."

"But so, like with piano. I should just give it up, you know? Because clearly I am not brilliant at it, so why embarrass myself?"

"Listen," Oliver said. "You know what I think? I think you and I have to get over that whole brilliant thing. Brilliant is for later. Brilliant is for critics, and they aren't going to agree with one another, anyway. If you love it, do it; follow where it takes you. Do your best. Brilliant or not won't be clear until you die, and then you won't care anymore anyway."

I laughed a little and moved to kiss him again. "Okay," I said. "It's a deal."

"And we will have to figure *this* out," he added, kissing my neck.

I pulled back a little. That sounded bad.

"Because," he whispered, looking into my eyes, "there is nobody like you, Quinn Avery."

"I'm a sleaze sometimes, too," I warned him.

"No doubt." He smiled. "What happened tonight?"

"I got mad," I said. "I got really angry, and all hell broke loose. It was a sight to see, as you predicted."

"I bet," he said. "Who were you mad at? Not me."

"No, you self-centered . . . At my . . . Oliver, is it okay if we sit down? I walked pretty far and I drank a truckload of beer tonight."

I plopped down.

Oliver laughed and sat beside me on a rock.

"What was I saying?" I asked him.

"Nothing. Why are you barefoot?"

"I lost a shoe. Her shoe. My mother's."

"And you taste like beer."

"Sorry."

"It's okay. Sometimes that happens."

I smiled at him. "Yeah. I guess so."

"And besides," he whispered. "You came here."

"Yes."

"I'm glad."

"Are you?"

"Yes. I am. And I'm glad you got mad. And I'm glad you survived it."

"Me too," I whispered.

"And now?"

"And now . . ." I whispered. "And now . . . I don't know. I'm still mad. But I didn't disappear so far. I don't know what happens next. What happens next? My parents send out the military to find me?"

"Your parents don't know where you are," he said, more than asked.

"No," I said.

"Quinn." He touched my lips with his finger, traced the shape of my upper lip, then the lower. His deep eyes closed and he lightly kissed the lips he had just anointed. "You know I don't want to let you go, but . . ."

"Yeah," I whispered. "I have to figure out how to go home."

26

OLIVER OFFERED TO WALK me in, but I asked him instead to drop me at the bottom of the driveway. I wanted to walk up myself. He insisted on lending me his flip-flops, but I left them in his car.

I walked barefoot in the waning dark up the long hill to my house.

I had a feeling my parents would be up, waiting for me, because, of course, when Mom went to pick me up at Ziva's at eleven, I wasn't there, and nobody there had seen me. It occurred to me that it would be good to have a plan of what to say, or how to behave, but nothing was coming to me, so I'd have to just wing it. I knew I was walking into fire.

I had no idea how huge the inferno was until I opened the back door.

Phoebe screamed. Allison said, "It's her, it's her. She's here. She's fine. She's okay," while Phoebe wrapped her arms around me and cried.

I peeked around the corner to gauge my parents' faces and saw there was a stranger in the kitchen with them—a stranger in a uniform. Or, no, not a stranger.

It was the police officer whose car I'd smashed into a few weeks earlier, the skinnier one, who'd spilled his soda. This was not a guy who was ever going to be happy to see me. "That her?" he asked.

Mom and Dad had both already jolted out of their chairs. They grabbed me. Dad's eyes were red from crying, and Mom's face was soaked with tears. I felt her fingers gripping me, hard.

"Sorry," I managed.

"Sorry doesn't begin to . . ." Mom held me away and stared at my face. "Quinn." A tear tore down her cheek. She shook her head and set her jaw. "We thought you were dead."

My heart pounded. I opened my mouth to object, to minimize—*I went to a different party! Can we not exaggerate? Allison sneaked out; did you call the cops on her, too?* But the lasers in Mom's eyes stopped me. I said nothing.

"They crashed," Allison whispered. "Mason and those guys. The cops were chasing them, and they went off the side of the road into a tree, and a bunch of the kids ran, but JD's in jail and Mason is in the hospital and so is what's her name, Adrienne?"

"Adriana?" My whole body went clammy. "Are they . . ."

"They're going to be okay," the police officer said. "Bumps and bruises—he's got a broken clavicle. She's got a concussion. They were lucky. You're the last one missing."

"Oh, my God." I slumped down onto the floor. Phoebe, in her cast, thumped down beside me, her arm around my shoulder. I noticed my bag on the kitchen counter, my wallet and cell phone beside it. On the floor were my white cardigan and Keds.

Mom's other shoe was standing glamorously in the center of the kitchen table.

"You caused us quite a bit of trouble, young lady," the police officer continued, shutting his black book. "Four officers are combing the town for you, thinking you could be wandering around stoned or drunk or drugged, being attacked, raped, wandering into traffic. It may feel like fun and games to you, but let me assure you, this is no joke. You put your own life at risk, and others' lives, too."

"Thank you, Officer," Dad said, thrusting his hand forward to shake with the cop. "We appreciate all you've done tonight."

The cop nodded briskly. "These kids have no understanding of—"

"We'll make sure she—" Dad started.

Mom interrupted: "Thank you, sir."

He took a look at my parents, standing there like a fortress wall between him and the three of us girls huddled on the floor behind our parents' legs. "All righty, then," he said, lifting his walkie-talkie from his belt. "I'll call off the search."

Allison whispered, "I'll text Jelly. She's a wreck."

"Thank you," I whispered. "Ziva, too?"

"Yeah, I think I have her number," Allison mumbled, thumbs working her phone. "Yeah, got it."

Phoebe hugged me again, lovingly, but also as a block so none of the adults would see Allison texting behind us.

"Let me get the door for you," Dad was saying. Mom stood with her arms crossed in front of us while Dad opened the back door for the police officer and shook his hand again, over the static of the police discussing me.

None of us budged until Dad closed and locked the door and came back to the kitchen. Only then did Mom turn around and grab me off the floor.

She hugged me tight again, then held me away from her and looked into my face with a fury that bordered on hatred.

"What the hell were you thinking?" she demanded.

"I don't know," I mumbled.

"You don't know? My brilliant daughter! You don't know?"

"No," I said. "I'm sorry. Obviously I am very far from brilliant. So hate me. I screwed up."

"And that's it?" she angry-whispered. "Three seconds of self-flagellation and it disappears now? Show's over and we should all just head up to bed like, 'Oops, sorry, burned a piece of toast'?"

"I don't know, Mom," I answered, getting mad again in spite of myself. "Why don't *you* tell *me*? You're the master. What should a person do after she screws up and humiliates her family because of her bad judgment and makes an ass of herself?"

"Don't you dare," Mom growled. "Don't you dare try to turn this around, miss. This isn't about me, as much as you might wish it were. This is about you, your choices, your behavior, the fact that I went to pick you up three goddamn hours ago but you were gone, were never there, and now you are standing in front of us like a pouty brat at two in the morning, stinking like a brewery and bleeding from the kneecaps."

"I thought we're the Avery Women," I muttered. "We just move the hell on. No?"

She stared at me.

Nobody moved.

"No," she said finally.

I blinked, twice. I wasn't sure what she meant. We don't move on? I don't get forgiven? She doesn't get forgiven either? Ever? We're not the Avery Women?

"No," she repeated, her voice hoarse. "We don't just move the hell on. That would be lovely, Quinn, but we don't. We can't. There's a price to be paid for bad judgment, for disappointing the people who trusted you."

"I know that," I said.

She nodded. "It's not easy to regain trust that's been shattered."

"True," I said.

"Contrary to what you may think, Quinn, neither Daddy nor I was ever under the illusion that you would be the first person to walk this earth error-free. You are a flawed person. We know that. Your sisters are flawed; Daddy and I, goodness knows, are rife with flaws—and you are, too."

"Obviously," I said.

"We're proud of you, Quinn," Dad interrupted. "We love all that you accomplish, and your quick, deep mind, your talents, your drive. But we love you beyond all that, too. We love you no matter what."

"This is how she gets in trouble?" Allison muttered.

"Allison," Dad warned.

"What, I'm just . . ." Allison put on a mocking voice. "'We love you, you're great, we love you. . . .'"

"We love all of you," Mom said. "No matter how impossible you make it sometimes. We love you. All. We love you so much it makes our hearts explode. It makes us want to die when we think you might be hurt, when we don't know where you are, when you take terrible risks. It makes us want to kill you."

"Sorry," I muttered.

"Good," Mom said. "You'd better be sorry. I never want to go through another night like this. We'll figure out how long you two are going to be grounded in the morning, after we hear every detail, but rest assured it will be for a long time."

I could hear Allison groaning beside me. I didn't budge. Mom looked at my face and sighed. "Listen," she said. "I know losing this house is hard. None of us wants to move, but we have to. I know you're angry at me, and disappointed in me. All of you."

"No," Phoebe started to object. "Mom, we love you—"

"I know you do." Mom cut her off. "But yes, you are angry, and embarrassed, and more. If you're not right now, you're going to be, and moving in with your grandparents is going to be really rough on us all. I did some things I'm proud of but also some that I'm ashamed of. I can't change what happened. Just like you can't change what you did. I have to live with myself, and at least for a while longer, you have to live with me, too. Not every day is going to be easy, or fun. But my failures are not excuses for yours."

She turned to me.

"Quinn, I want you to understand this. We are beyond angry at you. I am honestly furious about your lack of judgment and your piss-poor choices, not to mention you wrecked my favorite new shoes."

"Sorry," I said again.

"Damn straight. You'll replace them, for starters, and trust me, they do not come cheap." She clenched her jaw tight. "It's been our job for seventeen years to try to keep you safe, but also to let you find your own way. From the moment you left my body I've been saying good-bye to you. It's hard to let you fly, especially on nights like this. I want to stay in this house I love and lock you in your room and keep you safe there forever. But fly you will."

"I promise I'll never—"

"Sure you will," Dad interrupted, smiling sadly, tired lines notching the corners of his eyes. "You'll make mistakes, and you'll stumble, and you'll make a fool of yourself. We all will. You'd just better never pull anything like this again. Any of you. You hear me? Keep the disasters small, please, and non-life-threatening. I think that police officer has us on a special watch list of problem families."

"Great," Phoebe said. "Way for me to start."

"We're disappointed in you, Quinn," Dad said.

"I know."

"But we don't hate you. Despite how clueless you think we are, it honestly doesn't shock us that you are going to act less than brilliant sometimes."

"Or even," Mom added, "that you'd choose to binge on the whole damn buffet of supremely stupid things in one night."

"Actually that did shock me," Dad said.

I had to smile a little at him.

"All right, me too," Mom admitted.

"Okay . . ." I started. "So then . . ."

"So then," Mom echoed, "when you screw up, we'll be angry and disappointed, and we'll love you anyway."

I stood in front of my disappointed mother and didn't disintegrate into crumbs and blow away. I was a mess, dirt-smudged and reeking of beer, and she, that fallen colossus of my childhood, was my height in her bare feet, with chaotic hair and eyeliner smudges under her normally flawless eyes. She didn't look perfect or stunning or even particularly strong.

She was just Mom.

And when I leaned forward, she gathered me in her arms and held me until I stopped crying.

27

ON OUR WAY UP THE STAIRS, my sisters flanked me. Halfway up, Phoebe said, "I don't know how I got lumped in with all you flawed people. I was home watching TV."

"You'd better be grounded longer than I am," Allison told me. "I totally could have snuck in and not gotten caught if it hadn't been for worrying about you, you dork."

"Thanks, you guys," I said to them.

"Jelly texted back," Allison whispered, looking down at her phone. " 'Hallelujah with sprinkles on top,' she said."

I smiled. Oh, Jelly. "I owe her a huge apology tomorrow, too."

"Yeah," Allison said. "But she's a good friend. She'll accept it. She says . . . Here, you can read it: She says she's glad you made it home."

"Home," I said, at the top of the stairs. The white room was ahead and to my right, all gleaming and spotless. "Me too," I whispered. "It's good to be home."

"Were you in the car when it crashed?" Phoebe whispered.

"No," I said. "I made them let me out, and they drove off with my stuff."

"So where did you go, then? Have you just been walking?" Phoebe's face was puckered with worry.

"No." I dragged them toward my room. We huddled in the doorway, against the doorjamb. "I went to Oliver's."

Their eyes widened.

"Don't say anything," I whispered.

They swore they wouldn't. We heard Mom and Dad coming up, so they scattered to their rooms. I stepped through the doorway and closed the door behind me.

Okay, I told myself. This is the room I live in, for tonight, my room. Mine, but not mine. My room in my mind is a place I can't get back to. I miss it. It doesn't exist anymore. I'll keep it. I'll move, I'll move on, I'll keep moving.

There were open boxes empty in the middle of my floor, awaiting my stuff, which was stacked in piles. I went past them all, taking off my clothes as I went, and slipped naked between the cool white sheets.

I lay there thinking about what had happened and watching the sky slowly change colors until, just as the first hints of red appeared, I heard something tapping on my window.

28

Oliver.

He was standing under my window, pitching pebbles up to it.

I grabbed a sweatshirt and a pair of boxers, crouching on my floor until I had them on. Then I opened the window and knelt on the bed.

"Hi," he said.

"Hi," I answered. "It's not even dawn."

"I know."

I looked at him, standing there beneath my window, his hair still all sleep-tousled, the new day dawning around him as he tilted his face up to look at me, as if I was all he needed to see.

Me.

I yanked my old Chucks onto my feet and climbed out my window. I sat on the ledge, balanced there on the precipice, Juliet in high-tops.

"You okay?" he asked.

"I don't know," I answered honestly.

"Good place to begin," he said.

"Yeah," I agreed. "It is."

He blinked slowly and gave me that half smile I've loved all my life.

Feeling a smile spread across my own face to mirror his, I breathed in the unmistakable scent of morning.

Acknowledgments

WITH MUCH APPRECIATION, I THANK:

Amy Berkower, my guru, advisor, partner, agent, and friend.

Elise Howard and Rachel Abrams, who hear the heartbeats and see the footprints of these Avery sisters, and ensure it all makes sense.

The whole team at HarperTeen, for bringing it all together, including the fab shoes.

The booksellers, librarians, and teachers who champion books that tackle the real deal about growing up, and thereby quietly pry open the floodgates to new worlds of empathy every day.

Mark Mandarano, for the invaluable insights into the longings and life of a young musician, and for confiding, among other things, the secret joke within Beethoven's Quartet in F Major, Opus 135.

My friends, including Meg Cabot, Carolyn Mackler, Wendy Mass, Judy Blume, Avi, Carin Berger, Mary Egan, Lauren Lese, Bea Niv, and Chris Scherer—whose humor and solidarity are my oxygen.

My cousins, nieces, and sisters-in-law—a phenomenal collection of strong, kind, funny women the Avery girls would love to hang with.

Magda Lendzion, my friend, support system, and sister-of-the-heart.

My parents, who taught me and are still teaching me how to love wholehearted and full-out joyously, through screwups and triumphs alike.

And Mitch and our sons, whom I love so much it knocks me sideways. How I got lumped in with you brilliant people I have no idea, but because of you, I spend every day of my life knowing I am, as Jed Avery says, rich beyond measure.